VIP's Revenge

VIBE a Steamy Romance
Series #6

VIP's Revenge

Lynn Chantale

4 Horsemen
Publications, Inc.

VIP's Revenge
VIBE a Steamy Romance Series #6
Copyright © 2022 Lynn Chantale. All rights reserved.

4 Horsemen
Publications, Inc.

4 Horsemen Publications, Inc.
1497 Main St. Suite 169
Dunedin, FL 34698
4horsemenpublications.com
info@4horsemenpublications.com

Cover and Typeset by S. Wilder
Editor Blair Parke

All rights to the work within are reserved to the author and publisher. No part of this publication may be reproduced, stored in a retrieval system, or transmitted in any form or by any means, electronic, mechanical, photocopying, recording, scanning, or otherwise, except as permitted under Section 107 or 108 of the 1976 International Copyright Act, without prior written permission except in brief quotations embodied in critical articles and reviews. Please contact either the Publisher or Author to gain permission.

This is book is meant as a reference guide. All characters, organizations, and events portrayed in this novel are either products of the author's imagination or are used fictitiously. All brands, quotes, and cited work respectfully belongs to the original rights holders and bear no affiliation to the authors or publisher.

Library of Congress Control Number: 2022940449

Print ISBN: 978-1-64450-646-2
Audio ISBN: 978-1-64450-644-8
Ebook ISBN: 978-1-64450-645-5

Acknowledgements

Every book has a bunch of people behind the scenes who help. I'm always appreciative of my publisher, 4 Horsemen, and my editors. This time I want to say a special thank you to the owner and trainers at Top Performance Gym: Sam, Bill, Fran, Jen, Josh, Coyle, Troy, and Robin, thank you so much for your dedication and passion for giving those with a disability a chance at a real workout and not taking it easy on us. Thank you for treating us as people.

Table of Contents

Acknowledgements v
Prologue ix
Chapter One 1
Chapter Two 9
Chapter Three 17
Chapter Four..................................... 29
Chapter Five 38
Chapter Six 49
Chapter Seven.................................... 53
Chapter Eight 57
Chapter Nine..................................... 65
Chapter Ten...................................... 75
Chapter Eleven 82
Chapter Twelve................................... 91
Chapter Thirteen 96
Chapter Fourteen................................ 101
Epilogue 108
Author Bio...................................... 111
Book Club Questions 113

Prologue

Mr. VIP pushed his glasses more firmly on his nose and surveyed the two unconscious men on the floor of the makeshift prison. The shapes were blurred, so Mr. VIP stepped closer to the bars. His vision improved and he could see the men more clearly. One had shoulder-length sandy brown hair, with half of the strands obscuring the man's face. The other man, black and bald, was sprawled on his back, with stained, dried blood on the collar of his shirt.

These two men, Joshua Hastings and Avery Cheathams, respectively, caused him serious trouble, trouble which had cost him his opportunity to destroy two of the most influential blind women in the community. Perhaps without these two men mucking up his plans, Mr. VIP could finally get rid of the baker and the lawyer.

"If we kill them now, we don't need to worry about someone guarding them," a snide, masculine voice said.

Mr. VIP barely spared the man a glance. "Isn't he," VIP indicated the sandy-haired man, "the reason why you're in jail?"

"Well, yes."

"They're sighted, and they've foiled the plans I had for Penelope and Amelia. With them out of the way, I will be able to succeed in my plans."

"I'm telling you we should get rid of Hastings. He's crafty and a soldier." This was from the fourth man lingering in the shadows. "I'm all for you getting your revenge, but Hastings needs to die."

Now Mr. VIP turned to face the corner and the speaker shrouded in the darkness. "I appreciate your help, but I got this."

"I'm with him. Hastings has caused me nothing but trouble," the snide voice agreed. "The only reason you're free right now is because of me. I don't want these two dead; I want them to suffer. The best way to do that is to kill their women." He stared at the sallow-skinned man. He was already thin and haughty, but forced confinement lent a gray pallor to the man's face and made his body gaunter. "No one is forcing you to be here. You're free to go."

"Where am I going to go without money? That bastard," he stabbed a finger at Joshua, "took it all."

Mr. VIP smiled. "Then I guess we'll just have to ransom them off."

Chapter One

On any other day, the sweet scents of chocolate, vanilla, and lemon would be a comfort to Penelope Bishop. However, this wasn't any other day: this was the day her husband, Avery, hadn't come home, hadn't shown up to open the bakery at 4 a.m., and hadn't returned any of her texts or phone calls. So here she was, pretending all was well when her mind created one gruesome scenario after another. The only saving grace was the bakery was busy.

Penelope was too busy to worry, and somehow between customers and baking cookies, she managed. Avery hadn't come home last night, which was so unlike him, especially when he was supposed to open the bakery this morning. *Did something happen to him, and emergency personnel don't know who he is so they could contact me? Or did he decide married life wasn't for him anymore?*

She dismissed the last thought as quickly as it had come. Avery spent months wooing her, and he still found ways of making her fall in love with him every chance he got, like leaving little love notes in braille in her apron pockets or a single flower on her desk. His latest gift had been the pair of silver hoop earrings she was wearing now. She touched the jewelry, then went back to folding boxes. She then donned gloves and filled the boxes with several dozens of cupcakes.

Carefully, she stacked the boxes, then carried them to the window between the kitchen and the main portion of the shop. Laughter, the tinkle of chimes, and the occasional ding-ding-ding of the card reader filled the air. Just another day at PB&J Bakery.

The bakery had been in her family for four generations. The last thing she wanted to do was shame her family with a bad decision.

The only way her family had agreed to her running the business was to have an assistant. The fact she could manage every aspect of the bakery without sight was beyond her parents' comfort level. It didn't matter she'd spent most of her life in the kitchen before she finally lost her sight at 15; all that mattered was proving to her parents and herself she could maintain the profitability of their legacy. Hiring Avery was part of the compromise—and the best decision of her life. Somehow, with his self-assuredness and open mind, he made her days and nights normal.

But it wasn't a normal day at the bakery because Avery wasn't there. Penelope paused as emotion clogged her throat. She breathed deep to keep her emotions in check.

Where could he be? Is he lying in a ditch somewhere, dead or dying?

"Hey P? There's someone up front asking for you," a female voice called through the window.

"Just a sec," Penelope called back. She finished filling the cupcakes and then carried the boxes through the double swinging doors. "Becky, there's a couple trays of cupcakes that need to go into the case."

"I'll grab them now."

A hand touched Penelope, and she stopped.

"Right behind you," Becky said.

Penelope stepped forward and set the boxes on top of the display case. She pasted what she hoped was a pleasant smile on her face. "Who is here to see me?"

"Are you the owner?" a pleasant male voice asked.

"I am." She turned toward the voice. "What are you selling? You sound a little too old for the Boy Scouts' popcorn."

The man chuckled. "You've a good sense of humor. I can see why he likes you."

The first fingers of apprehension tickle her spine. She tucked her hand in her front apron pocket and closed her fingers around her collapsible cane. If all else failed, she did have a weapon at the ready. "To whom are you referring?"

"Oh, I'm sorry. Avery and I go way back. I just thought I'd drop in and see how he's doing." Something metallic clinked on the case. He must have placed his hands on the top. "This is a really nice place you have here."

"Yes, it is," she agreed.

"It would be a shame if something happened to it," he continued conversationally.

Penelope stiffened. "The last person who threatened me ended up in jail."

He chuckled. "Oh no, you misunderstood me."

"Then clarify," she said coldly.

The double doors squeaked as Becky came back out. "Got the cupcakes and I put the cookies on trays while I was back there. I'll bring those out in a sec."

The soft slide of the case doors and a cool blast of air floated along Penelope's right side.

"Gage Bedford will come in a little later and help me in the kitchen."

The doors slid close. Becky placed a hand on Penelope's arm. "Are you okay? You look a little pale."

"I'm good," she assured her employee. "Go grab those cookies, and I'll finish up here." Penelope waited for the swinging doors to squeak before she returned her attention to the man. "And your name?"

"I can see you are very busy." Footsteps retreated on the tiled floor accompanied by the jangle of keys. "I wanted to warn you."

Penelope had enough. She extended her cane and walked through the half door separating the case from the main floor, following the sounds of the man's progress. "Allow me to escort you from the premises."

The man gasped. "You're blind? Oh, Christ on crutches. He married a blind woman." He chuckled before it turned into a loud, boisterous laugh. "Too rich."

Who is this fool? Penelope wondered. *And how does he know Avery?*

"Penelope?" a younger male voice queried.

"Gage." She tried not to let the relief in her voice show. "Could you escort this gentleman from the premises and make sure he doesn't come back?"

"I wouldn't do that if I were you," the man cautioned.

"You heard the lady." Gage had steel in his voice. "Please leave before we call the cops. They usually stop in about this time."

"Very well," the man said. "You've made your choice. Tell Avery I was here. When he comes back." The chime on the door jingled. "If he comes back," he said, as laughter mingled with the chimes.

Penelope stood stock-still. *Was that the man's way of telling me he knows what happened to Avery?* She stepped forward. Gage caught her.

"Don't go after him. It's exactly what he wants."

"But he may have information about Avery," she protested. "Why would he say those things to me unless he knew what happened to Avery?"

Gage steered her down the hall. Tile turned to carpet and led her to a consult room.

"Listen to me. I was watching the man's face. He wanted to goad you into a reaction."

Penelope held out a hand, her fingers grazed the back of a chair. She sat. "He was with Joshua last night. Did Joshua make it home?"

"No."

For some reason that gave her some comfort. "So, they could be together."

"That's the assumption we're working with. You have cameras in the shop?"

"Of course." After all the vandalism and destruction to the shop last year, Penelope thought it more than prudent to update their surveillance system. Where before the cameras only focused on the cash register, the shop now had cameras on every area of the shop.

"Good. I'd like to get a still of the man to Sergeant Falls."

Penelope stood, stepped forward. The room spun, rushing up to greet her. With a gasp, she crumpled to the ground.

Amelia Bedford-Hastings fought the ever-present panic constricting her chest. She forced air in and out of her lungs. She had to stay calm and present. She had to be strong when all she wanted to do was curl into a ball and sob. If something had happened to Joshua, she would not survive.

A cold, wet nose brushed her elbow. Amelia tried to ignore the animal, but the dog persisted.

"Okay, girl," Amelia sighed. She swept a caress over the dog's silky fur; that one simple gesture eased the tightness in her body. She wasn't alone. She had Kiska, her guide dog as comfort. "You're right, girl; he wouldn't want me to fall apart. He'd want me to look for him. Besides, Penelope has to be going nuts as well. We have to be strong for each other."

Footsteps hurried in her direction. The scent of frankincense and man preceded a gruff voice. "I came as soon as I could," Dakota Mills announced, stopping in front of Amelia.

"Thank you, Kota." She swallowed the tears clogging her throat. "I know you were busy."

"Don't even apologize. This is Joshua we're talking about. We both know he wouldn't up and disappear unless he had no choice. Not after, well he doesn't go anywhere unless you know where he's going."

Amelia nodded. "I know he can take care of himself, but he'd have called or somehow gotten a message to me. He wouldn't change his plans without letting me know. Something really bad has happened to him." Even to her ears, her words were becoming more rushed and shriller. Very deliberately, she drew in a deep breath, held it in, and then slowly exhaled. When she spoke again, her voice was steadier. "Something has happened. And whatever has happened, Avery is with him."

"Avery?" Kota asked.

"Yes, Penelope's husband."

"Do they often hang out?"

There was scratching on paper, so Amelia presumed he was taking notes. "Yes. A few times a month, but I think Joshua and Avery were planning something."

"Like?"

She smiled. "If Joshua wanted me to know, he'd have told me."

"So, it could've been a surprise for you or . . ." He let the sentence hang.

"Anything," Amelia supplied. "Neither of them made it home last night."

Kota reached over to pat her hand, then stopped.

Amelia smiled, feeling the heat of his palm radiate above her skin before he withdrew. She bit back a smile. Kota remembered she didn't like to be touched, and she appreciated that. "With Rodney escaping, Joshua has been very vigilant about my safety, and when he leaves, he assures me of his return."

Dakota shifted on his seat, and clothing rustled. "Yes, Joshua mentioned the breakout. He's added additional security."

"And they've been wonderful. Half the time, I don't even know they're there."

"How's Darius working out? He's one of our newer recruits."

"He mentioned that." Amelia paused to compose her thoughts. "He's reserved, but pleasant. I can tell he isn't used to being around someone with sight issues."

Kota chuckled. "Most people aren't when you consider that only about 6% of Americans are affected." He said soberly, "Other than that, he's working well with you when he's here?"

"I've no complaints."

"Good." Kota resumed his questioning. "Has anyone contacted you?" he asked.

"Like for a ransom?" she clarified.

"Yes."

She shook her head. "We're both insured, but no one has said a word."

"All right. I'll start at the bar they were at last night. Do you know the name?"

"One of the microbreweries downtown." She extracted her phone from her pocket. The device spoke too fast for Kota to catch the words, but Amelia followed. "Kinsey's; it's about three blocks from Abigail's Place."

"I know where that is. It's big with the college kids. Hang in there, Amelia. We will find Joshua."

Chapter Two

Drip. Drip. Drip.

Avery Cheathams winced as his head pulsed in time to the rhythmic drips. Cold helped dull the ache but did nothing for the pain. He laid there, listening. Breathing. Assessing.

His forehead felt tight, as if he'd hit it on something hard and now had a knot. He quashed the urge to move and probe the area. Something stuck to his cheek and crusted over his left eye. It could be blood or dirt or both. Still, he needed to know where he was.

He'd only been in this type of predicament once before, as a teenager for an initiation, and he did what he had done then. He kept his breathing deep and even, as if he were still asleep. He didn't dare open his eyes until he could figure out where he was. Breathing, not his own, alerted him to someone else in the room. Slowly, the events pushed through his hazy brain.

Drinks at the bar with Joshua. The two were planning a celebration for Gage, his and Amelia's brother-in-law. Then the talk turned to BDSM—something he knew Joshua and Amelia were into, and something Avery and Penelope wanted to try, at least more than what they were currently doing in the bedroom.

Drip. Drip. Drip.

He had to be in a basement or some other damp place. Mold and mildew permeated the air. *But why am I here?* Again, he strained his ears for any other clues. No voices. No footsteps. He was alone, except for the man breathing near him.

In slow degrees, Avery shifted until he was facing the direction of the breathing. By going slow, his stomach didn't roll as bad as he thought it would, but his head made its displeasure known by setting off a vibrant thud that stole his breath. He laid there a moment, allowing the frantic pulsing to subside to something manageable. He then opened his eyes. Dim light greeted his bleary vision and was just enough illumination to make out the shape of his companion, Joshua.

"Well, damn," he muttered.

Avery crawled until he knelt next to the prone man and had to place a steadying hand on the floor to keep from toppling over. Breathing deeply helped stop the room from spinning. The change in position brought his attention to his face. Carefully, he touched the spot above his left eyebrow. He had a bump the size of a golf ball, along with a gash that was now crusted over. No wonder his head hurt. He rubbed the back of his neck, a bump there as well. *Somehow, we must have been drugged. But how?*

Avery shook Joshua's shoulder. "Wake up!"

Joshua groaned but did not open his eyes.

"C'mon, man. Wake up." Avery shook him harder.

There was no warning, only an explosion of movement, which had Avery flat on his back with a hand at his throat and a knee on his chest. Joshua glared at him with cold, unseeing eyes.

"It's me. Avery," he croaked. Some instinct warned him not to struggle.

Joshua blinked several times before his eyes cleared, and recognition washed through his irises. As abruptly as Avery had been grabbed, he was released. He drew in a grateful breath and waited for the black dots to disappear from his vision.

"Sorry." Joshua sat back on his heels.

Avery waved off the apology before rubbing the back of his neck. "Next time, I'll poke you with a stick."

Joshua flashed a wan smile. "Where are we?"

"Somebody's basement is my best guess."

Joshua helped Avery to a sitting position, frowning at the blood. "Did I do this?" He inspected the gash. "No. It's already crusted over. This happened last night." He ran a hand through his disheveled, shoulder-length hair. "What did we drink?"

"We didn't drink; we were drugged." With great effort, Avery maneuvered until he was sitting next to Joshua. They sat with their backs propped against the cold, cement wall.

"My mouth feels like it was stuffed with an old gym sock." Avery ran his tongue around his teeth in an effort to remove the grit. "Feels like it too."

Joshua nodded. "Yep. Definitely drugged."

Carefully, Avery made it to his feet, using the wall for an assist. Now that he was standing, the room spun and tilted. When he swayed, Joshua was there, lending an arm.

"Maybe you should sit down for a bit," he suggested. "You look like you've done a round or two with somebody's fist."

"Feels like I've gone around or two with somebody's fist," Avery agreed. He breathed until the nausea and vertigo lessened. Still, he allowed Joshua to help him sit back on the unyielding floor. Somehow, they had to find a way out of here. He pulled back his sleeve to glimpse his watch. He then checked his front pockets. Wallet was still there. The only thing that seemed missing was his cellphone.

"Hey man, you got your cell on you?"

Shifting and rustling beside him told him Joshua was looking. "Everything but," Joshua answered. "All my cash, cards are here. So are my keys." He held up a small ring with several keys on it.

"Me too."

Drip. Drip. Drip.

"Is that supposed to be some sort of torture? Make us thirsty, then let the water drip?" Avery quipped.

"We've got to get out of here," Joshua muttered more to himself than Avery. "Amelia will lose her mind."

"Penelope won't be too pleased either. I'm supposed to open the bakery this morning." He sighed. "Now she's going to use work as a way of not worrying about me." He scrubbed the heel of his hand over his face. Avery stood, swayed, and then clutched the wall to stay upright.

Together, they explored their prison: old cement walls, the floor sloped in one corner to accommodate a drain; a large bucket and a roll of paper towel sat near the drain.

Avery stared down at it. "Not exactly the Super 8 Motel," he quipped.

Joshua stood next to him. "I've been in worse." He touched the paper towel. "At least there's paper."

Avery snorted.

"There's a sink in the other corner," Joshua informed him. "At least we'll stay hydrated."

Avery walked to where Joshua pointed. He hadn't realized how thirsty he was until he heard the plop of water in the sink. He watched another drop drip from the faucet. A rust stain ran from the back of the sink where the plumbing was housed all the way to the drain. With a flick of his wrist, he turned on the cold tap. After a moment, he cupped his hand, dipped his head, and slurped. The first trickles of water down his throat washed away the grit and sandpaper. He could almost see his body reviving with each swallow of liquid.

"What did you do before you became a baker?"

Avery shut off the water, dragged his forearm across his mouth. "Before or after my misspent youth?"

Joshua grinned. "I can't see you as a misspent youth."

"Oh, I have one." He grimaced. "Drink some water. It will help clear your head." Avery again rubbed the back of his neck.

Joshua crossed to the sink, bent his head, and repeated the same thing Avery had done. The only difference, Joshua used a paper towel to wipe his mouth, then hung the damp towel over the lip of the sink to dry.

Avery studied Joshua a moment, then nodded. "Your color is better."

Joshua squinted at him before he drew his hair back into a messy ponytail. "You've got blood on your face and shirt."

"Yeah. I must have hit my head on something." Avery rubbed the back of his neck again.

"What do you remember from last night?" Joshua walked to inspect the hinges of the door.

Avery leaned against the bars facing Joshua. "The last thing I remember is going to the bathroom." He scratched the back of his neck. "Everything after that is a blur until I woke up here."

"You've been doing that a lot," Joshua said suddenly.

"What?"

"Rubbing the back of your neck."

"There's a knot of something back here that itches," he admitted.

Joshua motioned for him to turn around. Even in the dim light, he could make out something that looked like a burn or rash. "Looks like a stun mark of some kind. That explains the blood."

Avery turned to the bars and gave them a hard tug. Nothing moved. He stepped down a little farther and repeated the shake. He glanced up to where the bars met the ceiling and back down to the floor. This wasn't something recently constructed but had been there a while. He pulled his hands away, noting the coating of rust. He dusted his palms on his jeans. He looked at them again, but the rust remained. It was definitely ingrained in the bars. "Do you think this was someone's attempt at a dungeon or what?"

Joshua studied the bars, which more like what he'd seen on the front of prison doors. "I shudder to think this was someone's idea of a fetish." He shrugged. "But you know the saying, your kink isn't my kink."

Avery bit back a chuckle. "So it's the 'or what'?"

"Definitely." He tapped a bar with his toe. "I wonder how they found a basement with a ready-made prison cell?"

Shaking his head, he walked back to the sink and rinsed his hands. Now that he was more coherent, the faint tinge of rotten eggs filled the air. He cupped his lips and sipped but tasted sweet and clean. If he was smelling sulfur in the water, maybe they were a little farther south of Ann Arbor.

Avery used a sheet of paper towel and dried his hands and face before placing it over the sink to dry with the other. "They have well water around here or a really good filtration system."

"What makes you say that?" Joshua queried.

"Sulfur." He raised his hand to rub the back of his neck again and stopped. "Ah. Did they do the same to you?"

Joshua ran a hand along the back of his neck, feeling the same irritation. He nodded. "How do you know about the sulfur?"

"You know Cabela's off I-75 down in Dundee?"

Joshua nodded. The sporting goods store, one of the largest of its kind, housed an aquarium worthy of Rainforest Cafe. It also held several life-sized stuffed animals, from the extinct wooly mammoth to a few bears indigenous to the Michigan forests.

"Had some friends who lived in the area. Every time it rained or was wet, the whole area smelled like rotten eggs. The people had to get their water tanked in unless you grew up drinking sulfur water."

"Sounds like it would be hard on pipes, both for the house and the body."

Avery chuckled. "You do have a sense of humor."

"Don't go around telling everybody," he retorted. "So, anything in your misspent youth prepare you for breaking out of here?"

"Anything in your military career prepare you for getting out of here?" he countered.

Joshua grinned.

He opened his mouth to speak, and Avery shook his head. The man pointed up.

Somewhere, a door slammed in the distance. Wood creaked, as the low murmur of voices drifted through the floor. Avery stared at Joshua. "I'm not going down without a fight," he declared.

Joshua nodded. "Damn straight."

The men fixed their gazes on the far corner of the room. They blinked in the sudden flare of light. "Steady," Joshua murmured loud enough for Avery to hear.

Avery dipped his head in acknowledgement.

Joshua observed a glint of metal between the man's clenched fist and bit back a smile. If there was an opportunity, they would be in good hands for an escape.

A man's shoes, then his pants came into view. For a moment, the light was blocked by a medium-built body.

The scent of fried food drifted in the stale air, as did the rattle of a paper bag. When their captor came into view, neither man moved.

"You!" Avery gasped.

Chapter Three

Someone was calling her name. Penelope moaned, as something sour was waved beneath her nose. She fluttered her eyelids as the scent permeated her foggy brain. She sat upright with a start.

"Did I pass out again?" She grimaced.

"Scared the life out of me," Gage admitted. "If you hadn't come around, Becky was going to call 911."

Penelope blew out a breath. For whatever reason, she was now prone to fainting spells, which was another reason why Avery had taken to opening the bakery in the mornings. They figured she needed the extra rest to stave off fainting.

"Drink."

A cup of water was pressed into her hands. She sipped the cool liquid. It was then she realized she was no longer on the floor but seated on a small sofa in the consult room. She drained the cup, then handed it back to Gage. "Thanks."

"You sure you're good?" Concern oozed from every syllable Gage said.

"Yes. No need to call for help. My doctor is aware of my fainting spells."

"I'd still feel better if you got looked at. What would Avery say?"

She placed a protective hand over her belly. "He would rush me over to my doctor."

"Thought so."

After a clean bill of health from her doctor and admonitions to be more careful, Penelope stood in the middle of the commercial kitchen, listening. If she went home, all she would do was worry. If she stayed here at the shop, she could get a start on tomorrow's production. They could always use additional candies for the cupcakes, and she could bake additional sheet cakes to freeze. She could even make cookie dough. *Didn't Becky mention we are low on oatmeal raisin?*

If she went home, she would be surrounded in Avery's scent, and her home was now their home. Everything would remind her of him, and she was scared that all she would have would be his scent.

Slap-slap swish.

Penelope turned toward the swinging door and footsteps.

"Amelia wants me to bring you to the house," Gage said.

Penelope shook her head. "I need to go home," she muttered.

Gently, Gage grasped her elbow and steered her toward the back of the shop. "Actually, Amelia would love to have your company. Isn't there some saying about misery loving company?" he said lightly. "The two of you can commiserate."

"Ha. Ha." She dug in her heels. "You're not as slick as you think you are. I know you're trying to hustle me out the back so you can lock up."

"You're very perceptive."

She could hear his grin. "What if— "

"We're not going to play the what-if game today," Gage told her. "What we are going to do is head back to my place where you'll be safe."

"They have to be okay." Penelope resumed walking. She pushed through the swinging doors, checked her office door, and then stood at the back door. "There isn't another man on Earth like Avery."

Gage helped her into her winter coat. "I can't imagine what Amelia is going through. Not after thinking Joshua is dead and finding out he's alive." Penelope blinked back the tears burning her eyes. She was so emotional these days, probably all the extra hormones running through her system. Avery just had to be found alive and safe. And maybe she and Amelia could encourage one another. "All right. Let's go to your house."

Jaeden Fletcher enjoyed the look of surprised confusion on Avery's face. "Doesn't this bring back old memories?" he taunted. "When we both wanted to be part of that stupid club." He flicked one of the bars. "They kept us in a dog cage that time with no water or food." He shoved the paper bag through the bars. It fell on the floor at their feet. "Unlike last time, we will feed you."

"Who's we?" Avery demanded.

"Your wife is very beautiful," Jaeden continued, as if Avery hadn't spoken. "And the business you two have is doing very well. It would be a shame for all of that to end."

Avery lunged for the bars and managed to snag a handful of Jaeden's shirt to pull him close. Avery twisted the material at Jaeden's throat. "You leave my wife out of this!"

Jaeden pried at Avery's fingers, even as the material tightened, and he gasped for air.

"We were friends," Avery snapped. "What the hell is wrong with you?"

Footsteps crunched. Joshua shifted beside Avery. "Let him go," he said quietly.

Avery glanced at him. "What?"

"Let him go," Joshua said more firmly.

At the unmistakable sound of a shotgun being loaded, Avery froze. He looked up to find a man he didn't know holding a sawed-off weapon at them. With reluctance, he shoved Jaeden away. The man stumbled back, coughing and gasping.

"I told you not to get too close to the animals," the cultured voice intoned.

"Gentlemen." A third man appeared in the gloomy light.

"Well, if this ain't 'old home week,'" Joshua sneered.

"Tell me about it," Avery muttered.

Mr. VIP stepped forward. He glanced at the man holding the shotgun. "Guns are such messy business," he said. "They're locked up and not going anywhere."

"He tried to kill me," Jaeden snarled, rubbing his neck.

"When you gloat, do it where he can't reach you." Mr. VIP stared at Avery, then Joshua. "You see, gentlemen, once I've finished my plan, you will be released to my colleagues."

"And what are your plans?" Joshua demanded.

Mr. VIP smiled. "I'm going to kill Penelope and Amelia."

"I'm so glad you're here," Amelia said, as she tightly hugged Penelope.

"Gage didn't really give me a choice," Penelope answered ruefully.

Amelia laughed, as she led her to a nearby sofa. "Gage mentioned you fainted?" There was no censure in Amelia's voice, only concern.

"Just a little lightheadedness," Penelope said airily. "My doctor told me to ease off the stress."

"Understandable. You can see why I insisted you come stay with me."

"I believe Gage said we could commiserate together."

"Sounds like him," Amelia said dryly. "How are you holding up?" she asked once they were settled.

"Should I be asking you that?" Penelope said.

"Hanging in there," she admitted.

"I almost didn't leave my shop," she confessed. "With work, I don't have to think, but being at home, even your home…"

"Makes their absence even harder," Amelia finished.

"Exactly."

"It doesn't help that Rodney escaped."

"Why us? We never did anything to him. We were friends. At least I thought we were." Penelope shifted on the sofa. "Had the police said Sam was after me, I could see that, but not Rodney."

Sam Davis had been a suitor of Penelope's until she caught him cheating. He'd also tried to steal her bakery by sabotaging the business in order to sell it to a developer. He was currently serving time for his misdeeds.

"I don't like gossip," Amelia began, "but that's all I have at the moment. He lost everything to his wife in the divorce. His company, his reputation, his daughter, just everything."

"Well, that's no reason to kill people."

"It is for some. If from what I've gathered, he's got it in for any successful blind or visually impaired person. Since we're married to sighted people, like he was, well, it's probably his twisted logic way of saving us."

"That actually makes sense in a scary way." Penelope shifted again. "I can't imagine Rodney taking out both Avery and Joshua. Maybe one, but not both."

Amelia smiled. "Right, which makes me think he's not working alone." She lifted her head as if listening to a noise. "Sounds like Gage is on his way in with some refreshments."

"I could use something to drink."

"Hello ladies," Gage greeted. "I've got sandwiches, some soup, and a variety of candies from PB&J Bakery."

"You know my motto: chocolate first!" Amelia said with enthusiasm.

"What kind of soup?" Penelope asked tentatively.

"Chicken noodle and broccoli and cheese. If none of these are to your liking, I'm sure I can find another can of something or other you like," he offered.

"I'll take some of the broccoli and cheese with a sandwich," Amelia said.

Once they had their food, Amelia popped a chocolate candy in her mouth. Chocolate would always come first. It was how Gareth bribed her to eat in those early years. Sadness and grief had her lowering her head, so much loss over the last year. She was grateful for Joshua being alive, but it meant Gareth's death and, subsequently, Victor's.

A spoon clattered to the table, breaking Amelia's reverie. "Everything okay?" she asked.

"I'm sorry," Penelope sniffled.

"Is it the soup?" Gage asked anxiously. "The sandwiches? I can make you whatever you want. Or I can order something else."

Penelope shook her head, as tears slid down her cheeks. "I'm sorry. I know I should eat, but I can't help thinking that maybe Avery and Joshua don't have anything to eat. Here we are enjoying a meal, and they could be starving." Her voice broke on a sob.

At that moment, Avery and Joshua were scarfing down cold burgers and fries. They sat with their backs to the wall, keeping watch on the stairs in the far corner.

"Wanna tell me why your best friend and Mr. VIP have teamed up to make our lives miserable?" Joshua asked with a mouthful of fries.

"I have no idea why Jaeden teamed up with Rodney, but we can't let Rodney hurt our wives."

"He won't get anywhere near them," Joshua said with more confidence than Avery felt.

"How can you say that when we're in here?" Avery demanded, temper rising. "Penelope will be at the bakery every morning, and she has so much more to lose than..."

"No, you misunderstand," Joshua interrupted. "Amelia will have Penelope stay with her. My partner Kota will protect them both. I would never suggest you and Penelope have anything less to lose. I'm worried about Amelia. She thought for years I was dead, so I've tried very hard to make sure she knows where I am. She will no doubt have Penelope with her."

Avery settled back down at the explanation. "Jaeden's been to the bakery. That's the only way he could've seen Penelope." He set his half-eaten burger back on the wrapper. "If I know her, she probably showed him the door."

"Our women are strong," Joshua acknowledged. "Stronger than they need to be at times."

"We've got to get out of here."

"I'm in agreement with that. We know why Rodney has us here, but why Jaeden?"

Avery sighed. "I wish I knew." He picked up his burger and resumed eating.

"So, tell me about your friendship with him."

"Not much to tell. We were friends throughout middle and high school, and sometime in college, we drifted apart."

"No arguments you can think of? Any perceived slights?"

Thoughtfully, Avery chewed a bite of burger. "I had a crush on his sister, but nothing ever came of that."

"As in you didn't act on it, or he didn't know about it?"

"As in a quick fling. After we did the deed, we realized we made better friends than lovers. Soon after she was seeing some other dude during that time. What we had was a harmless flirtation, nothing more." He smiled at the memory. "Well more like an occasional hook-up. You know, the friends with benefits." He popped the last of his burger in his mouth, wiping his hands on a crumpled napkin. "After that, we lost contact with one another. I even think she got married."

"So, when's the last time you even spoke or saw him?"

"Maybe ten, eleven years ago."

"What was the initiation he mentioned? Gang or fraternity?"

Avery grinned, but there was no humor in it. "Ah, and there's my misspent youth. We wanted to be a part of this club back in high school. Growing up in the D, there were a lot of choices for me to make. I could join a gang, but really didn't care for the senseless violence, even though I did my share of juvenile things: stole a few cars, some shoplifting. Never got caught for those things. It was the initiation which sent me to the police. They got us for trespassing and property damage."

"Was anyone hurt?"

Avery shook his head. "Naw. We busted up some windows on an old restaurant, went in and tried to dismantle one of the fryers still in the kitchen." He smiled at the memory. "We were working on removing the manufacturer's stamp when we got caught. So there we are, me, Jaeden, and two other dudes." Idly, he scratched his nose. "That was the first time I ever rode in the back of a squad car. Needless to say, my parents hit the roof. They sent me to a different school and made sure I had plenty of activities to keep me occupied." He folded his hands in his lap. "You know, I don't think my parents ever ungrounded me from that incident."

They shared a quick laugh.

"But serious business, we paid a fine and community service. No one was hurt or damaged."

"That sounds harmless enough."

"Perhaps. Since Michigan doesn't do sealed juvie records, anytime I go for a background check, that incident shows up." He cast Joshua a sidelong look. "Kept me out of the Marines."

"You wanted the military?"

Avery nodded. "Spent six months with a recruiter, and he just couldn't make it work. So, I went on to option two: culinary school."

"And now you're part owner in a bakery."

"Penelope tried to give me shares in the business, but I won't take it. It's been in her family for years. It needs to stay that way."

"You're not the typical baker."

"Nope. What about you?"

"Graduated high school and two weeks later was sent off to boot camp. Worked my way through the ranks. A lot of what I did was, and is, classified."

"Then how did you and Amelia meet?"

"A fetish club. She was doing a rope demo with Gareth, and I had to meet her. The rest, as they say, is history."

"So how did they make Amelia think you were dead?"

"Got injured on my last assignment. Instead of her family telling her I was in a hospital, her half-sister Leigh, an attorney from Amelia's law firm, and Dawson Cahill conspired to steal Amelia's money."

Avery released a low whistle. "Damn, that's messed up."

"Yep. Leigh and Dawson tried to kill Amelia and the lawyer," Joshua rolled his shoulders. "He hurt Amelia in ways." He inhaled and exhaled, as he recalled the lines forever imprinted on her back. "So, I arranged for him to have special visits from a few special lifers for as long as I live while he's in prison."

"Remind me not to piss you off." Avery stood up and walked to the iron door. Squatting, he examined the lock. "I think I can pick this."

Joshua came to squat beside him. "Then let's do it."

Four men sat in four rickety, mismatched chairs. One, Jaeden Fletcher, held the clean, good looks of a born salesman; another, Rodney Kimbal aka Mr. VIP, wore thick lens glasses. The third man, Dawson Cahill, thin and sallow, glared down his long, thin nose at his companions, while the fourth man, Darius, plucked a piece of lint from the creased dress pants he wore. Of the four, he was the only one in a suit.

"I say we kill them now," Dawson Cahill said. "The longer we keep them alive, the more chances they have to escape."

"They must know the women they love are dead before you can kill them," the man in the suit responded. He leaned forward, eyes glittering with a rage that was palpable. "I don't care what you do with the baker, but Hastings must be made to suffer. He allowed my brother to suffer and die."

"Actually, having them live with the grief is a far better revenge than simply killing them," Mr. VIP pointed out.

Jaeden looked Mr. VIP up and down. "Who died and made you boss?"

"I've spent the last thirteen months in a 12x12 cell with sub-standard bedding and a steel commode, eating food not fit for human consumption, and fighting off the advances of too many to count. I'm not going back to that hellhole. I will get paid for my time."

Jaeden perked up. "Paid? There's money involved?"

"Didn't you see the long-haired fool? His wife is a millionaire. She will pay whatever it takes to get her husband back."

"Well, Avery's wife ain't rich, but she is pretty. Think I could get money from her?"

Jaeden caught the speculative gleam in Dawson's eyes. "What's your stake in this?"

"Actually, Penelope is pretty well-off," Rodney put in. "She may not have the type of money Amelia has, but the house Penelope owns is worth seven figures. The bakery, in its current location, is worth about the same. Take away her business, you take away her livelihood."

Jaeden nodded, as if he'd made up his mind. "Avery deserves to die for what he did to my sister."

Chapter Four

Joshua dozed as much as he could. He and Avery were huddled together in the corner of their cell for warmth in the damp, cold basement. They were thankful to still have their outer coats. Overhead, floorboards creaked. Joshua opened his eyes and listened. The creaks were tentative, as if the person walking didn't want anyone else to know where he was going.

"What is it?" Avery mumbled.

"Someone's coming."

A door swished open. Indistinct music rushed down the steps, along with the scent of melted cheese and stale beer. They waited for the overhead light to snap on, but it didn't. A rush of adrenaline zipped through Joshua as he readied for fight or flight. Beside him, Avery shifted, giving Joshua room if needed.

Joshua bit back a smile. Avery would be a great asset, and not one Joshua had to worry about.

He recognized the shoes on the tired wood steps. Joshua frowned. *What does he want? And why can I never remember the man's name?*

"Didn't he work for the Bedford family?" Avery murmured.

Joshua nodded as the thin, sallow-complexed man came into shadowed view. Lock up had not agreed with the man. Still, the man sneered as if he hadn't spent the past several months in jail. "So, you're behind this?"

"Partly," Dawson admitted. "How much is life worth, Hastings? Do you think she'll turn over her entire fortune for you, or leave you here to rot with your friend?"

"It's only money," Joshua drawled.

The thin face glowered. "Why do people with money always say stuff like that?"

"Because it's true. I'm not with Amelia for her money, which is a concept people like you can never understand. And yes, Amelia would trade all her money for me."

Something flickered in the depths of the man's irises. Had the light been better, Joshua would've been able to identify the emotion.

"What about you?" He faced Avery.

"I would be surprised if Amelia gave her fortune to free me," Avery answered.

Dawson rolled his eyes. "Your woman, you idiot," he snarled.

Avery shrugged. "We don't negotiate with terrorists." He flicked a piece of dirt from his pants. "Do what you will; our wives will not let you get away with this."

"Even if you're able to gain access to her money," Joshua began, "you wouldn't be able to keep it."

Fear skittered across Dawson's face before it was replaced with a scowl. "And why is that?"

"Because you won't be alive to spend it."

Dawson swallowed hard, his Adam's apple bobbing with the action. "That's tough talk for somebody in a cage."

"Who's really behind this?" Joshua demanded. "I know you're not smart enough to pull off a jail break and an abduction. Leigh and Chad are both in prison. Victor's dead. So, who's pulling your strings, Flawson?"

"It's Dawson," the man said through gritted teeth.

Joshua made a shooing motion with his hand. "Your name isn't important. You're just another minion, forgettable and disposable."

Seething, Dawson stalked as close as he dared to the bars. He stared into Joshua's face for a long time. "VIP is right; killing you is too easy. You need to suffer. I'll make sure Amelia's death is as painful as possible."

Joshua lunged, his fingers only grazing Dawson's skin, but it was enough to draw blood. Dawson placed a hand to his cheek. Without another word, he spun on his heel and stomped up the stairs.

"He really doesn't like you," Avery commented, settling back on the floor.

"The feeling is mutual." Joshua stared at the far side of the basement. He had no doubt Dawson would make good on his threats, but Joshua also knew no one would get close to Amelia and live. For a moment, a fleeting moment, Joshua had seen the surprise on Dawson's face at calling him out on not being the one in charge. If Rodney wasn't the mastermind or Jaeden, who had it in for him?

"Do you get the sense that we're a distraction?" Avery patted his pockets a few times, then smiled. He pulled out a pocketknife from an inside pocket. "With this and that file you took off Dawson, I think we can pick the lock."

"You saw that?"

Avery held up a key. "You think this is important?"

The men traded items. Avery went to work on the lock, while Joshua inspected the key. It was a brass number, thin with forked notches on one end and a rounded head with a hole drilled in the middle. "Looks like an old-fashioned bank key."

"I took it off Jaeden."

Joshua surveyed their prison.

Something in the corner near the sink caught his attention.

He walked over and stared up. The bars didn't quite meet the ceiling. He stretched his frame as tall as it would go, his fingertips barely grazing the top of the wall.

"Give me a hand with this," Joshua said.

Avery straightened, pocketing his makeshift tools. He watched as Joshua positioned the bucket close to the wall, then stepped on it.

"Whatcha find?"

"Let me see your knife." He held out his hand and closed his fingers around the metal once it was slapped in his palm. Carefully, Joshua worked the blade between the bars and the tiny seam. The mortar was old and broke easily. He turned his face away as debris crumbled away and drifted down.

Brick by brick, Joshua handed each down to Avery until he had a gap. He stuck his arm through the hole, all the way up to his elbow, and drew out a handful of cobwebs.

"It's a Michigan basement." Floorboards creaked overhead. "Quick. Give me the bricks." With as much speed and precision as possible, Joshua returned the bricks back to their original position.

The door swished open. Avery pointed to the pile of dirt. Joshua nodded, turned the bucket over and sat on it as Avery settled not far away, his back to the wall.

"How long do you think they can keep us here?" Avery said conversationally.

"Oh, as long as they can before our wives begin flooding the media with our disappearance," Joshua answered.

The stairs creaked.

"I've no doubt my partner is going over the bar's surveillance tapes," Joshua continued.

"There are a couple of cops who are chummy with the ladies. That Sergeant Falls is a nice guy. Met him when we had that nasty business with Sam trying to take over Penelope's bakery."

"Kota has contacts in law enforcement too."

The footsteps ran back up the stairs and the door slammed. Both men sprang to their feet.

"How long do you think we have before they come back?" Avery steadied Joshua as he climbed on the bucket once more.

"Don't know. But if we can get this wide enough, we can crawl out through the old coal chute." *However long it takes us to escape is far too long.* Joshua kept that thought to himself as he worked.

He and Amelia hadn't been reunited all that long, maybe a year or so. Before that, she believed him dead, and he'd been led to believe she hadn't wanted him when he needed her the most. No matter what, he had to get back to Amelia.

The doorbell pealed; both Amelia and Penelope stiffened at the sound. Kiska let out a soft woof.

"I'll get it," Gage announced.

"No, Mr. Bedford," a pleasant male voice contradicted. "Please stay with the women."

"Sounds like Darius," Amelia said, patting Gage's hand.

The phone rang. "I'll get that."

The women chuckled. "I really appreciate you inviting me here, even in my emotional state," Penelope said.

"Don't worry about it, P. It's better we stick together. And there's plenty of room."

"No," Gage snapped. "You can talk to me and tell me what you want."

At once, both women turned toward the sound of his voice. Amelia half rose from her seat. "Gage? What's the matter?"

"Sergeant Falls is here," Darius announced.

"This will go better if you tell me exactly what you want," Gage ordered.

Amelia skirted the couch, using Gage's voice as a guide. "Is that them? What do they want?"

"Get a trace started," Sergeant Falls ordered in a low voice.

"Amelia," Gage pleaded.

"Please. Let me hear what they want." She held out her hand for the phone.

For a long, tense heartbeat, Amelia didn't think Gage would give her the device. Finally, he relented and placed the cool plastic in her palm. Immediately, she placed it to her ear. "This is Amelia."

"If you want to see your husband alive again, you'll do exactly what I say," a stilted, mechanical voice ordered.

"I need to know he's alive now," Amelia countered. "And Avery too."

"Both men are alive," the voice confirmed.

Amelia felt a tug on her sleeve. She cringed and shook it off. "I need to speak with them before I commit to anything." She swallowed the lump in her throat and tried to ignore the painful pounding of her heart.

Something crackled over the phone. Amelia held her breath, straining her ears for every bit of sound. *Muffled voices. The scrape of shoes or is that a chair? Floorboards creaking.*

"Put it on speaker," came a hoarse whisper behind Amelia.

A button was pressed, and the handset removed from her fingers. Next, the phone was placed in front of Amelia.

"You're doing good," Darius told her loud enough for her to hear. "Keep them talking."

She nodded her understanding. Now there was the clomp, clomp, clomp of someone walking, no stomping, downstairs.

"Say something."

Silence.

"If you want to get out of this alive, say something."

"I'm coming home to you, Amelia, and tell Penelope I'm bringing Avery with me," came the honeyed Southern drawl.

Amelia gasped, gulping down the torrent of questions she wanted to fling at him. He was alive, and he was coming home to her. She swiped at the tears rolling down her cheeks. "Good to know."

"Stay safe, baby."

"That's enough!" the voice said. Now reverse stomping was heard, and Amelia used that moment to regain her composure.

"What do you want?" she said, once silence drifted through the line.

"I want five million dollars wired into my account. Once I have confirmation of the transfer, I'll release your husband."

"You'll release both men," Amelia told him.

The soft chuckle sent a shiver down her spine. "I'll think about it and call you back." The line went dead. Amelia sagged against the table, barely aware when Gage led her to a nearby chair. On her right, quiet sniffling met her ears. She reached out a hand and gripped Penelope's.

"They're alive," Penelope said between sniffles.

"They're coming home to us," Amelia said through her own tears.

"He was using a voice distorter," Darius pointed out.

"Did you get a location?" Sergeant Falls demanded.

"We've narrowed the signal to Scio Township. There's a lot of vacant places out there to hold someone."

"They're in a basement," Penelope spoke up.

"How do you know that?"

"You heard him. He went down some steps," she answered.

"He could've been on the second floor," Falls argued.

"Have you ever placed a phone on speaker in a basement?" Amelia asked.

"No."

"Try it sometime. The sound gets hollow and a little echo," Penelope explained. "They're being held in a basement."

"We need to discuss this ransom," Sergeant Falls said.

"We'll come out better if we can find where they're keeping Mr. Hastings and Mr. Cheathams," Darius said. "I doubt their abductors will keep them alive once they have the money."

Penelope gasped. "But we're giving them what they want." She stood up, placing a hand over her mouth. "I think I'm gonna be sick." Cane in hand, she hurried from the room.

"You could've been a little more tactful," Gage admonished. "There is no reason to stress Penelope more than necessary."

"Would you have me lie to her?" Darius demanded.

Amelia clicked her tongue. Kiska shook vigorously, along with the jangle of her tags. "C'mon girl. Let's check on Penelope."

Avery divided his attention between Joshua and the darkened staircase. "What was that all about?" The stack of bricks next to the bucket was growing.

"Buying us time." He scraped loose another brick and handed it down.

"I don't know about you, but Penelope doesn't have five million dollars hanging around."

Joshua squinted at him, then went back to removing the bricks. "I'm aware of that. I'm not willing for Amelia to hand over her fortune for me or you."

"Especially when we know they want to kill the women we love."

"So, we get out of here, open a can of whoop ass, and then get home." Avery cracked his knuckles.

Joshua hopped off the bucket with a grin. "That is the idea, my friend."

Chapter Five

"How many days do you come in at the crack of dark?" Gage stifled a wide yawn.

Penelope chuckled. "Every day I wasn't in school or away on vacation," she answered, flicking on the row of lights in deference to Gage. She also turned on the ovens and proof boxes. She was tugging on a large bin on casters when Gage caught up to her.

"Are you supposed to be pushing and shoving heavy stuff?" He deftly moved her out of the way and took over the canisters.

"It's on wheels," she answered, a touch of impatience in her voice. "I was slinging fifty-pound sacks of flour and sugar, not to mention the wedding cakes, before I even learned I was pregnant."

"And until Avery gets back, I'll do the heavy lifting or shoving as the case may be."

"I'm so afraid he won't," she admitted, as she crossed to the walk-in, pulled out butter, eggs, and a gallon of milk. These she set on the stainless-steel prep table, then went back for a bottle of vanilla.

"The men are resourceful. If there's any way they can escape, they will."

Penelope nodded. Tears burned her eyes and clogged her throat. She thought it best not to say anything else.

"What's next?" Gage asked, pretending not to see Penelope's tears.

"We have rolls that need to proof." She waved a hand to the walk-in. "There should be two racks covered in plastic. Just roll them right into the proof box." The proof box was a large, upright metal container, held at a humid, low temp ideal for yeast products. "Then grab the clipboard for today and work through the list. We did a lot of prep work last night for today."

They worked in silence. Soon the whir of mixers or a computerized voice announcing a timer or measurement punctuated the bakery.

The aromas of rising yeast, melted butter, brown sugar, and cinnamon were delicious.

"Do you know who that guy was yesterday?" Gage asked, scooping out cookie dough and placing the rounded mounds on parchment-lined sheet pans.

Penelope piped fluffy, fragrant chocolate buttercream onto the tops of cupcakes. "I think it's someone who knows Avery."

"I did give his description to Sergeant Falls."

"Good. Who knows, maybe he had something to do with Avery's disappearance."

A chime signaled the entrance of an early-morning employee. "Good morning!" Shay called. "I think I gained five pounds just by sniffing the air."

Penelope chuckled. "Morning, Shay. Come on in and see where Gage is."

The clomping footsteps halted. "You're not supposed to be here this morning."

Penelope could hear the censure in her employee's voice.

"That baby of yours is gonna come out looking like a swirl of frosting if you're not careful," she admonished.

"I'm fine, Shay," Penelope said.

"Have you heard any news? Have they found Avery?"

"Not yet," Penelope answered, refilling the pastry bag with more frosting.

"I also saw a police car posted out front. Is everything good?"

"Added security, since I refuse to close the bakery for any length of time." Penelope set down the bag, then transferred the tray she'd finished to the waiting rack, where she exchanged it for another tray of unfrosted cupcakes.

"So, they haven't caught that guy who escaped?"

"Until they do, police will be posted outside, and we'll have private security."

"Wait, Gage. You need to sprinkle the coarse sugar on the tops of those," Shay said.

"Oh. Sorry," he mumbled.

Penelope smiled as she listened to Shay explain the right way to dust the raw cookie dough with sugar. Tuning them out, she continued with the cupcakes.

She was still thinking fairly pleasant thoughts while she sat at a small, round table in the front of the store. Actually, she was more or less forced off her feet with a plate of turkey and Swiss croissant and several peanut butter cookies. This was the quiet part of the afternoon, after the lunch rush and before people got off work.

Before Avery, she never carried a cellphone, finding the devices too intrusive. Now she kept checking the device for any updates. Each time she brushed the screen on her phone, it merely announced the time.

"I'll be right back," Becky, her counter employee, called. "I want to fill a couple of the trays before we get another rush."

Penelope waved her hand in acknowledgment as she bit into the flaky pastry. For once, her stomach didn't roll and protest at the food. She was halfway through her lunch when the bells of the door twinkled and chimed.

"Take your time looking around," Penelope invited. "Someone will be with you shortly."

"You're so pretty," a child's voice gushed.

Penelope sat a little straighter. "Oh, you're so sweet. Thank you." Penelope stood, picking up her plate and carried it behind the counter. She placed it out of sight in a large, plastic dish tub.

"I was hoping you could help me," the child continued.

"What do you need?" Some warning bell tripped at the back of her mind. She strained her ears for any other noise, slowly realizing the child was by herself. "Are you here by yourself?"

Clothing rustled, and Penelope got the impression the girl nodded her head but couldn't be sure.

"Was that a yes?" she asked. "I'm blind, so you'll have to answer yes or no."

"You mean you can't see?" The little voice was incredulous. "What happened to your eyes? Did they get broken?"

"In a way," Penelope answered. "I was born with an eye disease that steadily got worse until I couldn't see anything anymore."

"Well, how do you make cookies and stuff?"

"I have scales and timers that talk to me. Where's your mom or dad?"

"Well, I was hoping he was here."

"What's your name, sweetheart?"

"Jamilah."

"Okay, Jamilah, was your mom or dad supposed to meet you here?"

"Well sort of. He doesn't know I'm coming to see him."

Penelope frowned. Which one of her employees could have a little girl trying to surprise him at work? She didn't have many male employees, and this girl was too old to be Gage's daughter.

The swinging doors squeaked. "I thought I heard voices," Becky trilled. "Who's your little friend?"

"This is Jamilah, and she's looking for her father," Penelope explained.

The case doors slid open and metal on plastic scraped, as trays were set into empty slots in the display case. "Give me a sec, and I'll look up and down the block for an anxious parent."

A moment later, Becky breezed past Penelope. The tinkling of the door chime signaled, and Becky went outside to look.

"Do you know your daddy's name?" Penelope asked.

"Yes. It's Avery. Avery Cheathams."

Avery and Joshua stacked the bricks to make it appear the wall was still intact. The ground squished beneath his boots, and Avery was glad he had on shoes. This part of the basement would definitely be in his nightmares for a long time. The number of cobwebs made him shudder.

"...ght the bucket, right?" Joshua asked some... ...very's left.

"Yes," Avery murmured. When they got out of this hellhole, he was taking a long, hot shower. Every time a web brushed his head, he had to resist the urge to flinch and swat at the wispy material. He had to fight his imagination from running rampant with thoughts of spiders and other creepy crawlies.

"Dammit!" Joshua exclaimed from somewhere ahead and to Avery's right.

Avery was careful to follow the path through the thick webs Joshua already broken. "What is it?"

"They boarded up the chute."

"Can we break through it?" Disappointment warred with hope. They were so close to escaping.

In the distance, a door slammed. They both looked up through the darkness and saw only clumps of webs. If they couldn't get out via the old chute, there could be another way.

"What about walking out the front door?" Avery suggested.

"There's at least three of them, and one is armed," Joshua mused. "We go home to our wives no matter what."

"Damn straight!" Avery echoed the sentiment. There was no way in the world he was going to let Rodney, Jaeden, or anybody else hurt Penelope, not when they were expecting their first child.

Carefully, they made their way back to the wall and took up century on either side of the bricks.

"When they open the cell door and come in, we'll knock the bricks on them and fight our way out," Joshua explained.

"I'm down with that."

Avery strained his ears, waiting to hear the telltale footsteps on the steps. *Will someone come down and check, or will they leave us alone for the night?*

Floorboards creaked, and a bit of dust drifted down. Some of the dust trickled into Avery's nostrils and stifled a sneeze. He rubbed his nose against his sleeve to clear away the debris. Another door creaked.

Someone was coming down the steps.

Beside him, Joshua tensed. Avery drew in a shallow breath, waiting.

Waiting.

"Oh, my God!" The voice was too low to make out who it was. "No way they're gone." Footsteps pounded, then faded.

"Wait," Joshua breathed quietly.

Avery nodded, not sure if Joshua could see the movement in the dimness. Soon more shouting was heard, and heavy footsteps overhead dislodged more grit from the floorboards.

Avery pressed his eye to a crack between bricks. There was just enough space to see two men come running down the steps.

"I told you the cell was empty," Jaeden said.

"Well, did you lock the door?" Dawson demanded.

"You were the last one down here!" Jaeden snapped.

"Amateurs. We're this close to a multi-million payout, and you're gonna throw it away for what?" Dawson pulled on the cell door, but it remained closed. "Get over here and open the door!"

"I don't have the key."

"Then maybe you should find it!"

Again, footsteps ran up the stairs. Avery pulled back from the wall. Joshua tapped him on the arm, and Avery glanced at him.

Joshua placed his mouth close to Avery's ear. "Follow me."

Avery nodded he understood. Joshua pressed the bucket handle into Avery's hand.

Metal scraping against metal drew his attention back to the other side of the wall.

"Took you long enough," Dawson sneered, turning the key.

Avery tightened his hold on the bucket handle, as Joshua shifted his weight from one foot to the other.

"How the hell did they get out?" Jaeden stepped to the open door, as Dawson walked into the space.

Bricks showered over Dawson as Joshua burst through the wall. He laid into Dawson while Avery jumped over the two men to Jaeden. Jaeden stumbled back, but Avery swung the bucket and caught his old friend on the side of the head. Jaeden grasped his head, blood spurting through his fingers. Avery swung again, putting all his weight, anger, and fear into the blow. The bucket split as Jaeden crumpled in a heap. For good measure, Avery kicked him. "Asshole."

Joshua came over to him. "Give me a hand." He reached down and grabbed Jaeden under the arms. Avery grabbed the unconscious man's feet. Together, they tossed him in the cell with a limp Dawson.

Avery picked up the key as Joshua sifted through the inert men's pockets. He came up with two cellphones and a set of keys.

"Lock 'em in, and let's get the hell outta here."

"It's been nearly forty-eight hours," Penelope began. She was still reeling from the earlier revelation, but without Avery there to confirm or deny, she didn't know what to believe.

Beside her, Amelia gripped her hand. From somewhere nearby, Penelope could hear Kiska, Amelia's guide dog, chewing on a squeaky toy. Every now and then, the object emitted a playful screech as it was bitten.

"Sergeant Falls," Amelia began. "They never called back to give me instructions on where to send the ransom. We know our husbands are alive. We've done everything you've asked of us."

"I hear a 'but' coming," Falls interrupted.

"Maybe we should bring in more help," Amelia suggested. "Kota is already invested because he's Joshua's partner."

"Swift Time could help," Penelope put in. "And I have no doubt my friends Moira and Violet will help. Moira would even take the next flight from Florida if I asked her."

"Penelope, you are absolutely correct," Amelia stated, as if Sergeant Falls hadn't spoken. "Call him now." She fixed her gaze in Sergeant Falls' general direction. "You've worked with Time before, right?"

"Yes, but I'd rather not have him involved in this right now?"

"Why not?" Penelope demanded. "Time was the one who caught Rodney the first time. If you don't let Time help, I'm gonna give my friend Moira a call. She'll definitely come up from Florida and help find Avery and Joshua."

"Ladies, I know you want to help," Sergeant Falls began. "But I'm here because I'm concerned for your safety."

"Whose safety?" Penelope asked suspiciously.

"Both of you," Sergeant Falls said. "Mr. Kimball expressed his intentions of ridding the world of all blind and visually impaired people, especially those who have successful businesses and are in mixed relationships. I believe you ladies fit the description."

"What did we ever do to him?" Penelope demanded shrilly. "My bakery always provided baskets and products for his company. And that makes me a target?"

Amelia patted Penelope's arm. "He's after me too."

Penelope turned toward Amelia. "But we didn't do anything to him. All we've done is work hard for what we have. No one gave us what we have."

"Penelope, I'm barely holding on," Amelia confessed. "I can't lose Joshua again. I wouldn't survive. Whatever the cost, whatever it takes to get our men home, I'll pay it."

"I can't let you do that," Penelope protested.

"It's only money. You and I both know we can't buy the type of love we have. Let me do this, and you continue to keep me company. If we're in danger, my house will be the best place to be."

"I can't just close up my bakery." Penelope was near tears. "There are too many people counting on the business. And we're headed into our busy season. My employees are more than just workers; we're family, and I have an obligation to take care of them."

"No one is asking you to close the bakery," Sergeant Falls soothed. "But we do need you to be cautious. Things worked well with having the patrols increased in the area, and you said you hired extra security."

Nodding, Penelope drew in several, deep breaths. "I'm sorry. Usually I'm calmer than this, but my emotions have been a bit erratic lately, which is why Avery was opening the bakery."

"How far along are you?" Sergeant Falls surmised.

"Eleven weeks," Penelope answered. "Avery is super excited. That's why I know something horrible has happened."

"We will find your men. Ladies, I know we've been over this before, but can you think of any reason they wouldn't come home? Or why someone would want a ransom?"

"Didn't you say Rodney Kimball escaped?" Penelope asked.

"And Dawson Cahill," Amelia said. "Dawson and my half-sister tried to embezzle funds. I could see Dawson abducting Joshua." Her voice broke on Joshua's name. "But I'll do anything to get Joshua back."

Penelope squeezed Amelia's hand. "We both will."

Running footsteps vibrated through the floor, then skidded to a stop in the family room a few feet away from the group.

"They've been found!" Kota exclaimed. "Avery and Joshua have been found."

Chapter Six

"You're not listening!" Joshua snapped. He fended off a uniformed paramedic, as she tried to wrap a blood pressure cuff around his bicep.

"Sir, please," the paramedic pleaded. The brass plate on her right pocket read E. Jennings. "Let me get your vitals, and then we can do whatever you want."

"No. Give me a phone so I can call my wife."

"C'mon Joshua, give the woman a break. She's just trying to do her job," Avery said from his seat. Another paramedic tended to the laceration on his head. Thanks to painkillers, the area was numb as the man applied stitches.

"The chief notified the police," Jennings told them.

"I need to speak to my wife!" Joshua's tone had no give. "If you want me to cooperate, give me a phone." The medic working on Aery paused long enough to dig a phone from his pocket and toss it to Joshua. "Did you want to call your wife too?"

Avery grinned. "Hell yeah."

Tires squealing on pavement drew their attention. Car doors slammed and murmured voices drifted through the firehouse doors.

"Where are they?" a familiar, feminine voice demanded.

"You said they were here!" This was from Penelope.

Avery half-stood before he remembered the medic giving him stitches.

The medic waved him on. "Go ahead. It can wait."

Joshua tossed the phone back to the man. Avery and Joshua hurried toward the voices.

The click-clack of nails, along with the slide of a white cane, greeted them.

"Penelope," Avery said, his voice breaking on her name. Tears burned his eyes as he hurried to gather her in his arms. He caught her to him, cinching her tight as he breathed in her fresh, clean scent. He'd never tire of her brown sugar and chocolate aroma. "Oh, my God, baby, I was so scared."

"Me too," she said between sobs. "Oh Avery. What happened?"

"Later. Just let me hold you."

"Lia." Joshua lifted Amelia, as she wrapped her legs around his waist. Her body trembled as her hot tears scalded his skin. "I told you I was coming home to you."

She nodded against his shoulder, squeezing him tighter.

"You shouldn't have come out," he chided gently. "You're safer at home."

"Not without you," she protested.

He smiled as he blinked away his own tears. He looked over Amelia's shoulder and found Kota scanning the room. Sergeant Falls stood a few feet away, shifting his weight from one foot to the other.

"Are you able to tell us what happened?" Sergeant Falls asked.

Joshua carried Amelia to a nearby chair. He sat with her in his lap. Promptly, Jennings was there with the blood pressure cuff. He sighed in resignation.

"What's that?" Amelia asked.

"Paramedic Jennings is taking my vitals. I was giving her a hard time before."

"I can see why," Jennings responded. "Your wife loves you very much."

Amelia skimmed her fingertips over the rough stubble shadowing his jaw to the tangle of his hair. She frowned when something sticky caught on her fingers. Joshua grabbed her hand and quickly wiped the offending webs away.

"Do I want to know?"

"Nothing a long, hot shower won't cure."

"So, what happened?" Sergeant Falls held a small voice recorder, then set it between the two seated men.

"Dawson Cahill, Rodney Kimball and..." Joshua began.

"Jaeden Fletcher held us in a house not far from here," Avery finished.

"Did they give a reason?"

"Rodney wanted us out of the way so he could get to Penelope and Amelia," Avery said.

"Dawson wants Amelia's money," Joshua answered. Amelia stiffened on his lap.

"He can have it," she mumbled.

"We don't negotiate with terrorists," he told her.

"What did this Fletcher guy want?" Sergeant Falls prompted.

"I don't know." Avery shifted in his chair, looked at Penelope. "He said he visited you at the bakery. Did he threaten you?"

"Not by words, but his demeanor was threatening. Gage showed him out."

"Did he put his hands on you?" Avery demanded.

Her soft smile was answer enough, as she skimmed her fingers over the taut muscle in his jaw. "No."

Avery relaxed. "How much longer? I'd like to get home and shower off the last two days."

"Just a few more questions. Do you know where you were kept?" Sergeant Falls then held up a hand as his phone buzzed.

"What's happening?" Penelope asked.

"Sergeant Falls has a call on his cellphone. And Paramedic Mike needs to finish stitching up my head."

She cupped his face with such infinite gentleness, tears threatened. He blinked them back. "We'll talk about everything once I get you home."

"Are you sure?" Sergeant Falls demanded.

The tension rolling from the officer was nearly palpable. Avery shifted Penelope aside, shielding her with his body, even as Paramedic Mike tied off the last stitch.

"What is it?" Avery demanded.

"Officers are at the dwelling in question now," Sergeant Falls began. "They've searched the premises."

"And?" Joshua prompted.

"There is evidence you two were there."

"Spit it out, Falls!" Joshua ordered.

"No one was there. The two men you say you left in the cell are not there."

Chapter Seven

Where the hot water rejuvenated and soothed his taut muscles and made him clean again, Avery was looking forward to only one thing: being skin to skin with the woman he loved more than his life. He padded back into the bedroom, not theirs but a guest suite in the Hastings estate. He paid little attention to the lush surroundings. Instead, he focused on the sexy woman with skin like vanilla custard. Penelope sat cross-legged in the middle of the king-size bed, wearing some filmy, see-through nightie that revealed more than it hid. Before he was halfway across the soft carpeting, he was hard and ready.

He had a glimpse of a slate and stylus, a portable device she used to take or make notes in braille, before she slid it beneath a pillow at her back.

"Avery," she began.

He pressed a knee on the bed, watched her throat swallow as if she was working up the courage to say something. He encircled one ankle, reveling in the smoothness of her skin.

"I need you, Penelope," he said huskily.

Desire leapt in her irises, and she touched her tongue to her lips. "Are you sure?"

Wanting her was the only thing Avery could be sure about at that moment. Slowly, he worked his fingers up her leg. She shifted, granting him better access, and he was pleased to see she wore no panties. He needed as much of her as he could get.

He kept his movements gentle, controlled. He didn't want to hurt her or the life growing inside her, the product of so much love, but right now he needed his wife, his woman, his mate. Lips replaced fingers, and he indulged her first moan. He skimmed her neatly trimmed folds already slick and wet with her desire for him. He dipped his head, tasting and teasing. She pressed more into him.

"Avery," she released his name on a breathless moan.

He teased her dewy folds with his tongue, losing himself in the taste and scent of her. He sucked her tight little pearl until she whimpered. However, he didn't want her to cum just yet. Reluctantly, he placed a last kiss on her swollen sex, then pressed a kiss to her navel. She shifted restlessly beneath him, unfulfilled and wanton.

Avery palmed one breast and licked the nipple of the other, remembering at the last moment how sore she said her breasts were. He didn't want to cause her any additional pain, only pleasure. She'd suffered enough over the last couple days.

Finally, he claimed her mouth. Soft. Supple. Submissive. He reveled in her sweetness, her texture. Avery savored every moment of his lips on hers, the slide of her skin, the scent of her arousal.

She touched him, as if sensing he needed as much closeness as she could give. Her hands never stopped roaming his body. She touched his face, his head, his back, his buttocks. Anywhere her hands could reach, she touched.

Avery lifted slightly, positioning his hardness at her entrance, rubbing the head until it was slick with her heat. Slowly he entered her, guiding his cock until she arched against him, urging him forward.

He closed his eyes as her heat enveloped him. Once he was balls deep, he rested his forehead on hers and simply held her.

"God, I love you," he murmured as he withdrew, then eased back in again. He kept his strokes long and languid. There was no sense in hurrying. He would never hurry through loving her again but would make this last, make it good for her as if he would never see her again.

Every ounce of love, protectiveness, and fear he poured into his lovemaking. Only when he felt her tight muscles grip and massage his hardness did he allow himself the luxury of a climax. Breathing hard, he settled beside her, still locked within her depths. He didn't even want to relinquish their most intimate joining and twined his arms around her to hold her close.

Penelope wasn't sure how long they laid together. All she knew, and cared to know, was Avery was next to her. The strong thunk of his heartbeat beneath her ear assured her he was real, solid. She breathed in his scent, well, their combined scents, and snuggled closer.

"He taunted us," Avery said. "Every chance Mr. VIP had, he told us how he would kill you." Penelope brushed a kiss across his chest, the damp hairs tickling her skin. "I was safe. Amelia made sure of that."

"I need to thank her for her friendship. She truly went above and beyond." They fell silent. "I don't know why Jaeden decided to drug and abduct me and Joshua. Well that cat Dawson made it clear with his ransom demand, but not Jaeden."

Penelope tried to pull away, but Avery's arms tightened, unwilling to release her. Instead, she ducked her head so he couldn't see her face.

"What is it?" he prompted.

"I think I know why Jaeden is mad at you."

When she didn't continue, Avery shifted their positions until she was sprawled across him. He cupped her face, and she leaned her cheek into his palms. She'd almost lost him and now what she had to say would certainly crush him. And, of course, he would do the right thing because that's the type of man he was.

Avery kissed her cheeks. "Baby, you're crying."

"You have a daughter. That's why Jaeden is mad at you."

Chapter Eight

"I can't believe this!" Mr. VIP kicked an ottoman from his path. The squared furniture skittered across the floor. "I spent months putting this breakout into motion, and the two of you go and fuck it up! Now how am I supposed to get close to Penelope and Amelia?"

"We didn't know there was a space behind the wall," Jaeden whined. He held a bag of melting ice to his swollen face. Not only was his lip split, and a gash above his eye, but he'd lost a tooth and should probably seek medical attention.

"They tricked us," Dawson sneered.

Mr. VIP swung toward the sallow, thin man. "And I thought you had some sense! Had I known you were so greedy, I'd have left your sorry ass in jail."

Dawson stood toe to toe with Mr. VIP. "You better watch your mouth, old man."

Mr. VIP whipped his hand back and smacked the other man across the face. When Dawson jumped back to his feet, Mr. VIP was ready with a small handgun. "I have nothing left to lose and killing one more person won't bother my conscience."

"The last man who pointed a gun at me died in an explosion."

Mr. VIP gave a careless shrug.

"Nobody mentioned any guns," Jaeden said nervously.

"Nobody gives a damn about you killing a bunch of blind folks," Dawson jeered. "I want my money." With that, he lunged at Mr. VIP.

Mr. VIP shifted, but not enough to ward off the attack. Dawson grabbed his wrist holding the gun, as both men fell against the wall.

"Stop it!" Jaeden shouted.

Mr. VIP wasn't willing to relinquish the gun. He'd been humiliated once already, thinking of the spanking he received at the hands of Father Time. His finger tightened on the trigger and didn't care which way the muzzle was pointed. He jerked his finger.

The crack wasn't as loud as he thought it would be. No more than a mild pop, like someone popping a balloon. Dawson jerked. Jaeden screamed.

Mr. VIP kept pulling the trigger until only the pall of cordite and ringing in his ears were the only sounds heard.

Avery held Penelope long into the night, stroking her long, thick hair, a combination of auburn she adored and about six inches of dark brown hair. Since learning of her pregnancy, she hadn't colored her hair. He buried his nose in the mass, breathing in the soft brown sugar of her shampoo.

He couldn't believe he had a daughter, especially not one as old as the little girl Penelope described. Absently, he stroked Penelope's spine. Sure, Avery had a fling with

Jaeden's sister, Jenna, early in college, but they'd used protection every single time. He always brought his own condoms, not trusting anyone for a minor but significant detail.

There was no way she'd have his kid and not tell him. Sure, they'd broken things off after a few months, but she would've told him. Wouldn't she?

And for Penelope to learn he may have a child he never knew existed when they were expecting their first baby...

"I shouldn't have told you," Penelope murmured sleepily.

"Did I wake you?" He pressed a kiss to her hair.

"We'll figure this out, Avery."

"I wouldn't have deceived you, P. I love and respect you too much for that."

She skimmed her lips over his bare chest. "You've told me about past relationships and anything else I wanted to know about you. I know you wouldn't have kept a child from me. I also know you'll do the right thing if she is your daughter."

"The right thing at the moment is to make sure my pregnant wife gets some sleep. She's been way too stressed the last couple of days."

"Shay is opening, and the security guard will be there as well as the police." She snuggled closer. "Not knowing what happened to you was the worst. All I knew was you'd find a way home if you could."

Avery squeezed her a little tighter. "I don't know what screw came loose in Rodney's head, but he is bent on killing you and Amelia. I couldn't let that happen, not as long as there was breath in my body. I waited and looked too long for you. I'm definitely not giving you up without a fight. Until he's back behind bars, I'm sticking to you like a shadow."

"Good, cause I don't think I'm ready to let you out of my sight yet."

Amelia could not sleep. Even though Joshua surrounded her with his scent and strong arms, she feared if she closed her eyes, he would not be there when she woke up. He was so still. To anyone else, it would appear he was asleep. She knew better.

Carefully, she circled one nipple. The tiny hairs tickled her fingertips. She traced the edge of the muscle to the small indentation, a long-ago scar from a bullet, before delving lower to the patch of skin on his side. She couldn't quite remember how he'd gotten this scar, but it was the texture of a cheese grater.

Joshua shifted, giving her better access to his body. Where she had needed the confines of rope or the scintillation of pain to ground her, she offered him sensuality. She wanted, no needed, to know and convince not just her mind but her body Joshua was still here.

"Lia," Joshua breathed in his honeyed drawl. "You have to sleep."

She shook her head, her hair grazing his belly as she scooted lower, pushing the sheet down as she went. Everywhere her fingers touched, she followed with her lips and tongue.

His small intake of breath assured her he was very much real, and they were together in bed. Muscles flexed and bunched beneath her palms. His body was always a welcomed contrast to hers, where she was soft and curvy, he was hard and lean. A fine dusting of hair trailed over his six-pack to this neatly trimmed pubes. She brushed a hand over his engorged penis. A trickle of moisture coated the head, and she swept her tongue over the surface.

In response, he fisted a handful of her hair. The small bite of pain galvanized her. She needed to overwhelm her sense with him: not only with taste, but his crisp, masculine scent, his warm, hard body, and the spicy taste of him coating her tongue. Slowly she swallowed him, alternating sucks with long, slow licks.

He was always so controlled, so careful with her, especially now. Amelia cupped his balls, fondling them and then gently squeezed until his fingers tightened painfully in her hair. She hummed her approval. She longed for the taste of him to slide down her throat, but she needed more. She released his cock with a wet pop, kissing and teasing her way up his body.

She straddled his thighs, guiding his cock to her slick entrance. He grasped her hips, and she took him in one steady motion, a sigh of satisfaction eased from her lips.

As if sensing what she needed, Joshua let her set the pace. He raised just enough to draw her mouth to his. Bodies entwined, mouths fused, all she could do was bathe in Joshua. She didn't want this to end. If she could make their loving last forever, she'd never have to worry about him leaving. He would always be in her, around her, against her. The climax caught her off-guard, and still she embraced the rolling orgasm, riding up one wave and down another, as she milked his cock. He shuddered beneath her, clasping his arms and holding her close. She sprawled over him, panting.

"Go to sleep, Lia. I will be here when you wake up," he promised.

Wailing, banging, and shouting jolted Penelope to an upright position. Avery pulled her close. He smoothed a hand over her hair, then down her spine.

"You're okay," he murmured. He didn't want to admit the noise had also scared the daylights out of him too. Now that the adrenaline was fading from his bloodstream, the dull ache of pain pulsed through his head.

She clung to his biceps, struggling to bring her rapid heartbeat to some sense of normalcy. One thing was uppermost in her mind: Avery was still here.

Avery pulled her tighter, not liking the trembling of her body against his. The noise had truly startled her. He swept a kiss along the delicate shell of her ear. "I'm here, sweetheart. We are safe in each other's arms." He wasn't sure if he said this for his benefit or hers. Either way, the words had the desired effect, and she relaxed against him. For several minutes, they held one another, just breathing. Somewhere the distant slam of a door preceded heavy footsteps. Muted voices could be heard, but the words indiscernible. Something was up. Avery checked the clock on the nightstand. It was barely four in the morning; nothing good ever came at four in the morning.

"Will you be okay while I see what's going on?" he asked.

She nodded. "Yes, if you take me with you." His mouth curving on her cheek preceded his soft chuckle. "I'm not ready to let you go."

"Grab your robe, and we'll see what's going on."

Penelope allowed Avery to guide her down the sweeping staircase, across the marble tile, to the family room, where voices were floating into the hall. "Something's wrong," Penelope muttered.

"I imagine it isn't good news at four in the morning," Avery agreed. He tucked her hand more securely at his elbow.

"Oh good, we were just going to send someone to wake you," Joshua greeted, as they stepped across the threshold.

Avery shifted, placing his body in front of Penelope's and the rest of the room. Her fingers tightened in the material of his shirt at his back.

"Is there something wrong at the bakery?" Penelope demanded. "Did an alarm go off and no one contacted us?"

"No. No," Joshua said quickly. "Your bakery is fine and the employees safe. They found Rodney."

"I need to sit down," Penelope said, as Avery guided her to the loveseat opposite Joshua, Amelia, and another man Avery knew as Kota. "Amelia, Joshua, and Kota are in the room," he said to Penelope.

She nodded her understand and threading her fingers through his.

"What happened?" Avery said, once they were settled.

"There were reports of shots fired," Kota took up the narrative, his deep voice held weariness, but was still strong. "After the police searched, they found a man now identified as Rodney Kimball, shot multiple times."

Penelope gasped, covering her mouth with her free hand.

"Oh. Is he still alive?" Amelia ventured.

"Unfortunately, yes," Kota said.

"Does his daughter know?" Penelope asked suddenly. "This has got to be so devastating for her."

"Forgive me if I'm a little less empathetic; the bastard has been neutralized, and there's one less crazy out there trying to kill Amelia and Penelope," Joshua snapped.

"At least he won't be coming after either of our wives," Avery agreed.

"But his daughter is innocent," Penelope insisted.

"She is, but Winifred is the catalyst for Rodney's killing spree," Amelia interjected quietly. "If I ever get the chance, I'm going to slap that woman silly. Too many good people died because of her selfishness."

"Be that as it may," Kota interjected. "Mr. Kimball is currently in surgery and his two associates are still at large."

Chapter Nine

The next afternoon, Avery stepped into the narrow foyer of Father Time Detective Agency. He unbuttoned his jacket and loosened his scarf. He'd known Swift Time for a while, and if he wanted answers to this question, the semi-pro wrestler-turned-PI was the way to go.

Sure, he could've asked Joshua for help, but the man had enough on his mind with making sure Amelia and, in turn, Penelope were safe. Avery could ask Time for help, even though it pained Avery to do so.

"Are you coming in or going to stand out there all day?" the deep baritone called.

Shaking his head, Avery turned the knob and stepped into the office just big enough to turn around in. There was a metal file cabinet to his left, a closet door to his right, and when he took two steps inside the room, he was at the only visitor chair in front of a postage stamp-sized desk. An older man with silver white hair, beard, and mustache grinned from behind the desk. Weak light filtered through the blinds behind the older man.

"How are you?" Concern colored the older man's tone. "I've seen you looking better."

Self-consciously, Avery touched the stitches on his forehead. "I've been better, but glad to be home."

Time nodded. "Joshua and his crew have the situation well in hand." Time studied Avery a moment. "But that's not why you're here."

"No, it isn't." He waved a hand to the chair. "May I?"

Time nodded.

"A little girl came to the bakery while Joshua and I were imprisoned." Avery plucked at the fringe on his scarf. "Her name is Jamilah, and I need to know if she's really my daughter."

Time stroked his beard. "And if she is?"

"Then I will take the time to get to know her." Avery sat on the edge of his seat. "I want to know why her mother never told me, if Jamilah is indeed mine."

Time pulled a legal pad toward him, drew a pen from the holder, and removed the cap. "Tell me what you know, and I'll get started with it today."

"He fucking shot himself!" Jaeden exclaimed. He paced the length of his living room. Since fleeing from the old farmhouse where'd they'd kept Joshua and Avery locked up, they had little choice as to where they could hide out. This three-bedroom home wasn't his, but a vacant property his real estate firm managed. The new occupants were still weeks away from closing. No one would think to look for them here.

Dawson winced as he shifted on a wooden stool. One bullet grazed his side; it was no longer bleeding, but it hurt like hell. "Not all the bullets found him."

"This was not supposed to happen." Jaeden continued to pace.

"What did you think would happen when you decided to abduct a grown man to avenge your sister? That he'd roll over and play nice?" Dawson shoved to his feet; angry spots of color slashed his pale cheekbones. "I'm not going back to prison. The Hastings owe me millions, and I intend to collect what's mine." He stood in Jaeden's path, glaring into the other man's eyes. "So, either grow a set or I can put you out of your misery."

Jaeden read death in the depths of Dawson's irises. "My sister is dead because of Avery. Had she not met him, I wouldn't be raising my niece right now."

"And where is this niece of yours?" Dawson eased back on the stool with a sigh.

"My parents. They say Avery isn't the father, but I know it's him."

"How do you know that?"

"His name is on the birth certificate.""

"That doesn't make him the sperm donor, just legally responsible for the child," Dawson scoffed. "DNA don't lie."

"But."

"I spent years working for the Bedford family and making sure I would receive a multi-million- dollar payout. I'm not leaving until I get what's mine." He stared hard at Jaeden. "Now, are you helping or pursuing some petty family drama?"

Jaeden scrubbed a hand over his face. If he could get a cut of the money, it would go a long way to helping his parents raise Jamilah. "Fine, but I want a cut."

Dawson's sallow face split into a mirthless grin. "Done."

Even though Avery retained Father Time, Avery sat behind the desk and typed Jaeden's name into a search engine. He hadn't seen the man in a good ten years, and his sister in the same amount of time. He scanned the results for the correct name. With the advancement of technology and so many people wanting to be found, the Internet was better than the old-fashioned telephone book for locating people, places, and things.

Avery was mildly surprised to see Jaeden had Facebook and Twitter accounts. He clicked on the FB hyperlink, and there was Jaeden smiling in a crisp business suit. He scrolled down the page, learning the man was a real estate agent, and a pretty successful one, if the amount of sold banners were any indication. A post halfway down the page caught his attention. Avery sat back, a small gasp of sorrow escaping his lips.

He clicked on the link, hoping he didn't need to be a friend to view the entire article.

"Jenna Jenkins lost her long-time battle with uterine cancer. She was laid to rest ..." Avery scanned down to the part of the obit where it listed those left behind. It listed her mother and father, her brother and two sisters, and a daughter, but not a spouse or significant other.

Avery leaned back in his chair, placing his hands on his head. He had to know. He cast a quick glance at the open doorway, but he couldn't leave Penelope unprotected. Could he risk traveling to her parents' home in an effort to learn Jamilah's true parentage?

Then there was Jaeden to consider. The man was still out there, waiting to hurt him or Penelope or both for whatever perceived slight against his sister. Sighing, Avery closed down the browser, but not before he located her parents' address.

"Penelope," he called as he rose.

No answer.

He skirted the desk to walk into the bedroom. He found his wife sprawled on top of the bedcovers; one palm rested on her abdomen while the other was flung against his pillow. Her chest rose and fell with each breath she drew. Love so potent and strong washed over him. His wife. His love. His heart. His best friend. He wouldn't wake her. Instead, he settled in the bed next to her, inhaling her sweet fragrance of chocolate and brown sugar. He could so easily have lost her. He placed his hand over hers, still able to see the faint burn that marred her skin.

The burn was a reminder of the fire someone tried to kill her with last year. Sam, her ex, always maintained his innocence at the fire and grudgingly Avery believed him. The only other person who could've possibly hurt Penelope was Rodney.

But why?

Because Penelope was successful and had a relationship with a sighted man? Could it be something as simple as that? That Penelope flourished where Rodney hadn't? Cool fingers squeezed his. He looked down to find Penelope looking up at him.

"I think I fell asleep," she murmured sleepily.

He pressed a kiss to her lips. "I'm glad you did. You were tired."

She shifted until she snuggled next to him. He closed his arms around her. "I'm so glad you're safe."

He kissed her temple. "I'm very glad you're safe too," he agreed. "Would you take a drive with me?" he asked after a while.

"Sure," she answered without hesitation. "Where are we going?"

Avery hesitated. "I need to know the truth about Jamilah. The only way I can do that is to speak with Jenna's parents."

"This must be so hard for you."

"What will I do if she's mine?" He hated to ask the question, but he needed to know if Penelope would still be there for him, for them.

"You mean we?" she countered. "You're not in this alone."

He swallowed the sudden lump in his throat. Her generous heart humbled him.

"I've met the little girl. She's sweet, and if she is yours, she will make a great big sister."

Joshua stood in front of the balcony doors, staring across the wide, uninterrupted blanket of snow. Several of the pine trees sported a dusting of the white stuff. He shifted his gaze to the left. The ruin of a workshop no longer sat on the concrete slab. In its place was a new building, one Gage used as a music studio. Joshua leaned forward, resting his forehead on the cold glass. He could just see the edge of a roof at the far end of the property. He blinked. *Is that a stream of smoke coming from the chimney?*

The moon slipped from behind a cloud, giving enough illumination for him to see it was only a cloud moving passed. But he wasn't so sure.

A familiar scent wafted through the air. He sniffed, trying to identify the smell. Behind him, Amelia gasped.

Joshua whirled, his hand going for the weapon at his back. He darted his gaze to the closed bedroom door, windows, and ceiling before returning his scrutiny to her very pale face.

"What is it?" Just to be certain, he walked the room, opened the bedroom door, and looked up and down the corridor. Satisfied no one was lurking in the shadows, he closed and re-locked the door.

He crossed to Amelia and placed a light hand on her arm. "Baby, you're trembling. What's wrong?"

Amelia opened and closed her mouth several times, but no words escaped. Instead, tears trickled down her cheeks.

Joshua drew her to him. She resisted, stiffening in his arms. He simply held her.

"Talk to me," he kept his voice soothing. "What is it?"

The scent of cedar, leather, and sandalwood was so strong, Amelia fought for control.

She clutched his arm so hard, her fingers bit into the muscle and he winced.

"Gareth," she breathed.

Joshua pulled Amelia to him. "Oh Lia." He stroked her spine, hoping to ease the tension from her body.

She shook her head, dislodging the messy ponytail from her hair. "I can smell him," she gasped.

Joshua opened his mouth to soothe and sniffed the air. He scented the cedar and sandalwood too. "I do too." He didn't see how that was possible when the man was dead. Just before Gareth Bedford died, he'd found Joshua. Even Gareth believed Joshua to be dead, but it was Gareth who'd been murdered in a tragic explosion. Now the man's preferred cologne was wafting through the house.

"Maybe Gage has a bottle of Gareth's cologne?" Joshua said.

"Gage is at the bakery."

"Where's Kiska?"

At the sound of her name, dog tags jingle jangled. A cold, wet nose brushed Amelia's outstretched hand.

"Maybe one of the guys is wearing it," Joshua mused. "Kota and Ric are on watch today."

"Dawson knows the grounds," Amelia reminded him. "He was privy to all the estate's secrets." She rested her head on his chest. "They used to torment me with your scent."

Joshua stilled, not sure he'd heard her right. "Say that again?"

"Leigh and her minions used to spray your cologne around the house, or that idiot who attacked me in the club. They figured out scent was the best way to trigger my anxiety attacks."

"You don't have as many attacks anymore."

She shook her head. "I had a few while you were missing," she admitted.

He brushed his lips against the faint scar at her hairline. "Not to be cheesy, but nothing but death will keep me from you," he vowed.

She held onto his shirt, breathing in his scent. "And hopefully we will be alive for a very, very long time."

They stood there, secure in one another's arms.

"If I give him the money he wants, would he leave us alone?"

"No," Joshua answered without hesitation. "Men like Dawson get off on hurting people and knowing you gave in once to his demands would only have him coming back for more when the money ran out."

"So much death." More tears dripped from her lashes. "I never wanted the money and would still give it all away."

Joshua kissed her forehead. "Which is why your grandmother and Gareth made sure you can't give away your inheritance." Even as he spoke, a flash of light caught his peripheral.

"What is it?" Amelia asked, as Joshua went still in her arms.

With an arm around her shoulders, Joshua steered them toward the balcony doors. He hadn't imagined the light, nor the smoke. "There's a light in the cottage."

"What cottage?" Her voice held a trace of wariness.

"The one Gareth shared with Victor."

⁓

Avery stared up at the two-story house, which reminded him of a saltine cracker box. The decorative shutters on either side of the house's windows needed a coat of paint, while the smoky gray siding could use a power wash. The sidewalk and drive were shoveled and salted. Slowly, he turned off the car.

A warm hand settled on his thigh. "We don't have to do this today," Penelope said.

Avery covered her hand with his. "Our lives could change again." He raised his hand to her lips and brushed her knuckles. "Something or, rather, someone I had a fling with years ago could cause you to hate me for the rest of our lives."

"As hormonal as I am now, the last emotion I feel is hate toward you. Avery, I love you with every beat of my heart.

We pledged to love one another for better or worse. We've had worse, and we've had better. Nothing could be as worse as not knowing if you were alive or dead. You stood by me when Sam was trying to destroy the bakery for his selfish purposes. This is me standing beside you, daughter or no daughter."

"All right. Let's go find out what we can."

"You're the last person we expected to see," WillaMae Jenkins declared, once all were seated in the living room.

"We wanted to talk with you and clear up some misinformation," Avery began. "Allow my wife and I to extend an overdue condolence for Jenna."

WillaMae waved her hand, as if dismissing the sentiment. "No need for that, son. Jenna wouldn't have wanted it."

Avery smiled at this. Indeed, the Jenna he knew didn't believe on dwelling on the bad. Life was meant to be lived, not wallowed.

"Why are you here now?" Clarence demanded.

"Jaeden got in touch with me. He believes I'm Jamilah's father."

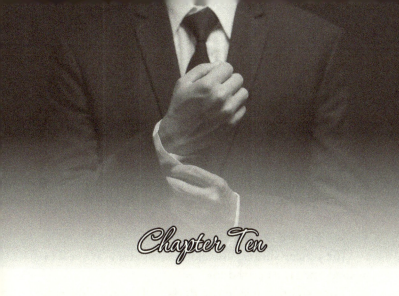

Chapter Ten

Swift Time wasn't sure why he needed to be at the hospital when he should be working on Avery's case, but Time knew enough to trust his instincts. If this was any other night, he'd be at the bar with his wife Abigail, but he needed to be here.

Carefully he worked his white cane back and forth across the industrial linoleum floors. To him, there was no definition between floor and neutral-colored walls. The only contrast he found was when he passed was when he came to an intersection. There, he paused long enough to read the signs attached to the walls.

As he approached the ICU unit, more equipment lined the walls. Large windows provided an unobstructed view into each of the patient rooms from the nurses' station, situated in the center of the wing.

Time spied a uniform officer outside of one room and headed for it. The officer straightened as Time neared.

"Help ya?" the officer asked in a voice not helpful at all.

"Falls has given me permission to see him," Time said, undeterred by the tone. "Swift Time."

"You got some ID?"

"Sure," Time dug in his pocket for his wallet. "This must be a boring assignment for you," Time began as he held out his ID. "Standing outside some scumbag's hospital room."

"It's not too bad," the officer said, his tone relaxing. "The nurses are pretty." Paper crinkled as the officer wrote. "I've got your name down."

"Thanks." Time returned his ID to his wallet and pocket. "Do you know if he's awake?"

The officer shifted, his clothes rustling. "Nope." He pushed open the heavy door.

Time stepped inside the darkened room. Slowly, he made his way to the bed. Monitors bleeped, burped, and dripped. Resting his cane in the crook of his arm, Time settled his hands on the raised bedrail. Rodney Kimball looked small and frail against the stark white sheets.

Oxygen hissed as the antiseptic, some citrusy cleanser, and adhesive wafted through the air. Beneath that was the faint odor of death. All the modern miracles couldn't stave off the inevitable.

"What happened to you, man?" Time asked softly. "There were so many other options for you to choose. You didn't need to take this road."

Time leaned closer. The man's once caramel-colored skin was now a sickly gray. Even the man's lips had lost all color. "You hurt so many people, destroyed so many families. And what about your daughter? Did you even think of how your actions would forever affect her? How will she live down the fact her father was a serial murderer?" Time sighed. "Well, none of that matters now. You won't get to hurt anyone else, and it seems like you're not long for this world either. Good-bye, Mr. VIP."

Without a backward glance, Time left the room. He'd just made it to the elevator when lights flickered, and his ears rang. He didn't fight the vision, instead embracing the vignette that played through his mind's eye like an old movie clip.

Two men. A house. A red-haired woman pointing a gun.

Time was jostled from behind.

"Excuse me," came the strained voice. "I'm so sorry."

"No problem," Time said, as the doors slid open. He stepped into the empty car. If he had a few more seconds of the vision, he could've seen what happened with the woman and the gun. He knew two women with red hair, and they could both be in danger.

"What is this place?" Jaeden demanded, looking around the spacious cottage. Slowly his brain calculated the worth: open, airy rooms; real hardwood flooring; crown molding; the custom exotic wood cabinets and granite countertops. This building alone would fetch an easy six figures, if not seven.

"My former employer's love nest," Dawson sneered.

"Interesting," he drawled. "Why are we here?"

Dawson pulled out drawers, rummaged through the contents, before moving on to the next. "There's a safe on the premises. It has cash and passports."

"You're looking for a safe in a desk drawer?" His tone was incredulous.

"The key, you idiot," Dawson snapped.

"Well, you can't find anything in the dark." Jaeden flicked on a nearby lamp.

"No!" Dawson snatched the offending cord from the wall and knocked the lamp on the floor. It fell with a crash and shatter of glass. "Now they know we're here."

Torn between wanting to find the key to a safe where plenty of cash was stored and fleeing to pursue another day, Dawson swore.

"I'm continually cursed with morons and idiots," he seethed. Dawson picked up the broken lamp.

"I hear voices," Jaeden hissed. He turned in time to take the heavy lamp to the face.

"Grams!" A little girl with dozens of French braids with beads on the end came barreling into the room. "I need some pictures for my family tree project." She stopped, looking at the newcomers in the living room. "Hey I know you. You're the bakery lady."

Penelope smiled. "Yes. How are you, Jamilah?"

"Good. How did you know where I lived? Did you follow me home?"

"No," Penelope said with a laugh. "Did you forget I'm blind?"

"Oh. Right. So have you seen my dad?"

"Jamilah, this is, was," WillaMae corrected, "a friend of your mom's. He stopped by to say hello."

"My mom went to heaven when I was six."

"I'm sorry to hear that," Avery stated. "You look just like her."

The little girl beamed.

Avery studied the round face for any of his features but couldn't see any, not in the shape of her lips, ears, or nose. Jamilah definitely had her mother's eyes.

"So did you find my dad, Ms. Penelope?"

"Is that what you went in the bakery to do?" Clarence asked.

Jamilah turned to her grandfather. "Uncle Jaeden said my dad worked in the bakery." She stuck out her lower lip in a pout. "I just wanted to see him."

"Oh sweetie, you know your dad is overseas right now. He's supposed to call you later this evening," WillaMae explained.

"But Uncle Jaeden said Avery Cheathams was my father. Not the other man."

Both Clarence and WillaMae tossed Avery apologetic looks. Beside him, Avery threaded his fingers through Penelope's. Now he was going to hear the truth.

"No, Jamilah. Your father is in the army. You know that. You even got to travel with him and your mom before she passed," WillaMae said.

Jamilah frowned. "But Uncle Jaeden promised me he would bring my dad home so I wouldn't be alone anymore." Tears bubbled and spilled. "He promised to bring me a new dad." She ran from the room.

"I'll talk to her." Clarence stood and followed the little girl out.

Avery swallowed the lump in his throat, while Penelope sniffled. "Seems like Jaeden has a lot to answer for," Avery said lightly.

"I'm sorry, Avery. Jaeden hasn't been the same since Jenna died. I remember when you and Jenna broke up. We were devastated of course." She offered a nostalgic smile. "We thought you'd be a part of the family. But when Jenna brought Gideon home, we knew she'd met her soul mate." WillaMae stood, crossed to a bookshelf, and retrieved a framed photo. She handed it to Avery.

"They married three months after they met. Jamilah was actually born on a base in Japan."

"I read her obituary. It didn't mention she married."

"Gideon works in some classified areas. He didn't want to draw attention to his family."

Avery studied the framed photo of the woman he had a fling with all those years ago. She was smiling at a plain-looking man in a T-shirt and camo pants. They both had their arms around a tiny baby swaddled in a pink blanket.

"That was taken shortly after Jamilah was born."

"She's not mine," Avery sighed.

"No. I'm sorry if this has caused trouble for you and your wife," WillaMae said. "I don't know what Jaeden was thinking."

"Grief does weird things to people." A door closed in the distance. "Will Jamilah be all right?"

"Children are surprisingly resilient. Her father wanted her to have as stable a childhood as possible. So, during the school year, she lives with us and during the summer, she's on base wherever he happens to be."

"Thank you. We won't take up anymore of your time." Avery stood, cupping Penelope's elbow as he rose.

He was helping Penelope into her heavy coat when his phone rang. Saying their good-byes once more, they exited into the frigid cold. A light dusting of snow had fallen since they were inside, but nothing overt. Avery held the car door open for Penelope. Once she was inside, he closed the door and then entered the driver's side.

"Are you okay?" Penelope asked.

"That was a lot of information to digest," he answered truthfully. "On one hand, I'm glad I'm not an instant father, but my heart grieves for that little girl." He leaned over, cupped Penelope's cheek. "I'm still reeling at how we're going to be parents."

"You didn't tell them what Jaeden did."

"They were already dealing with so much. They'll soon know what Jaeden has been up to. No since in worrying them right now."

The cell phone rang again.

"Yes?" Avery answered.

"Are you and Penelope together?" a honey-drawled voice demanded without preamble.

"Yes. Has something happened?"

"Jaeden was found in the cottage at the edge of the property."

Chapter Eleven

"Lia. I need you to stay here," Joshua shoved as much authority into his voice as he could.

"You only get to use that tone of voice when we're doing a scene," she snapped. "I am not waiting in our room alone while you go off and investigate."

Joshua almost smiled at her bravado. She was right. While she was his sub in the bedroom, it didn't always translate so well to outside. "Lia, this is for your protection."

Amelia placed a hand on his chest. "Where you go, I go. They made it onto the property even with all the security. What's to stop Dawson from coming into the house to hurt me or you for that matter?"

"Lia, I would not survive if something were to happen to you." He pulled her close.

"Nor I you," she returned. "If I'm with you and the rest of the security team, it's highly unlikely Dawson will come after me."

Joshua searched Amelia's face for a hint of a lie. What he read was sincerity, love, concern, and determination. He leaned his forehead against hers. "You do exactly what I say," he conceded. "And bring your guide."

By the time they reached the cottage, emergency personnel were loading a still-unconscious Jaeden onto a gurney. An IV was taped to the back of his hand, while gauze was wrapped around his head. A paramedic kept pressure on the wound. "Looks like Jaeden has some blunt force trauma to his face," Joshua told Amelia, as they went up the walk. He continually scanned the area and found three of his security men lurking in the shadows, but nothing else.

"What was he doing in the cottage?" she mused, allowing Kiska to guide her up the slight incline to the front door. "Halt," she said, once they entered the foyer.

The faint scent of leather, cedar, and sandalwood hit Amelia hard. Beside her, Kiska whined, pushing her wet nose against Amelia's hand. "I'm okay," she assured the animal.

Gentle fingers skimmed her arm. "Lia?"

"It still smells like Gareth," she confessed. "I miss him."

Joshua placed an arm around her waist. "Come away from the door."

Since Gareth and Victor died over a year ago, Amelia hadn't had much need to visit the cottage, other than to supervise the packing up of their belongings. Other than that, she hadn't been in the dwelling since, so the details of rooms were a little fuzzy in her memory. Beyond the front hall, she couldn't remember how close to the windows and other rooms were.

"I'm going to put you in the corner of the living room closest to the hall," Joshua explained, as he led her to the corner. "You are out of the line of windows and doors, and I can see you from anywhere on this floor."

"And if I need a quick exit?" she prompted.

"You can either go out the front, or your guide can lead you across the room to the back door."

"Describe what you see?"

"Desk drawers are pulled out. Papers are strewn across the desk and floor. There's a broken lamp and glass on the floor."

She listened as Joshua's footsteps receded.

"Mostly it looks like they were searching for something."

Amelia worried her lower lip. "Gareth kept a key to his safe, but I have that now."

"What did he keep in the safe?"

Shrugging, she said, "I never asked. I presume important papers. Probably cash or other documents he wanted stored."

"Where's the safe?"

"Bedroom."

"Do you have the key with you?"

Amelia dug beneath her shirt for the long chain. Besides the collar, this was the only other necklace she didn't take off. On the long chain were two wedding bands. One was large and a little warped; the other was an eternity band of diamonds. Between the two was a flat skinny key in the shape of a long U. She handed these to Joshua.

"I don't think there are any biometrics on the safe, but you will need both bands along with the key to open it."

"Is there a combination?"

She offered a small smile. "Your birthday."

⁓

Joshua crossed to the bedroom and was surprised he could still see Amelia from this vantage point. It wasn't until he entered the large walk-in closet that he lost sight of her. He wasted no time in finding the face of the safe and had to wiggle the large band on the stem, as it was warped and didn't want to sit right. He placed Amelia's band and pushed the post. It slid in to reveal the keyhole. He inserted the key. The door clicked open on an ordinary combination. He did the left right left thing and the second door opened.

He expected to find cash or envelopes with important documents. What he didn't expect was a letter addressed to him.

He swept a hand inside and found nothing else. He relocked the safe, then returned to the living room.

"Who else knew about the safe?"

"Victor knew, but he couldn't open it without me or Gareth present."

Joshua deftly looped the chain with its rings and keys back over Amelia's head. "And the last time you opened it?"

"When we cleaned out the cottage. There should be an inventory list in my office. Did I miss anything?"

"There was a letter addressed to me inside."

For the first time in three days, Penelope and Avery stood in the foyer of their home. The welcome scents of fresh baked bread, chocolate, and cinnamon warmed the air.

"It's so good to be home," she breathed, shrugging out of her coat, then hanging it on the coat tree. She toed off her boots before setting them on a small wire shelf for that purpose and donned a pair of fluffy slippers to continue her trek across the marbled tile. "Smells like Mrs. Hubbard has been busy."

"Probably worried about us." He slipped his arms around her waist as he kissed her temple. "You don't think she called your parents, do you?"

Penelope shook her head. "She waited until we got you back to let them know what happened. Believe me, I got an earful when I finally spoke to them. They were ready to liquidate any and all assets to assist with getting you back." Her voice hitched on the last part of the sentence. "They know how happy you make me and are a valuable part of the family."

Avery cleared the lump from his throat. "You make me equally happy." They stood there a moment. "I couldn't have asked for better in-laws than your parents. I'll call them once things settle down a bit more."

Penelope untangled from his arms. Unerringly, she made her way through the open doors of the dining room to the kitchen beyond. She ran her fingers on the cool surface of the counter as she made her way to the stove. She found the kettle, filled it, and then set it on the front burner. The electronic ignition ticked before it whooped into life. She adjusted the flame.

"Looks like Mrs. H left us some banana bread, and it has chocolate chips in it."

Avery moved around Penelope, adding dishes and silverware to the eat-in counter.

"Are we safe here?" Penelope asked, for the first time, doubting the four solid walls of her home could protect them.

"The alarm is set. There's an armed security guard. Beyond that, both Rodney and Jaeden are in the hospital. There is no reason for Dawson to come after me or you," he assured her. "His beef is with Joshua and Amelia."

"That still didn't stop him from abducting you."

Water roiled in the kettle, and Penelope readied a couple of mugs. The kettle would steam and whine any minute.

"When they had us in that basement cell, I saw Dawson's face. He wanted to hurt Joshua as much as possible. Knowing Rodney was going to kill Amelia after extorting money from her was exactly what he wanted."

"I don't understand how a human being can hate someone so much." The kettle shrilled. Penelope turned off the flame and poured hot water into the two waiting mugs.

"I wouldn't have thought my long-ago best friend would blame me for his sister's death. Or try to brainwash his niece into thinking I'm her father, but it happened."

"What did Joshua say happened?"

Avery sat down in one of the padded high-back stools at the counter. "He believes Dawson attacked Jaeden. I'm sure he could get more information, but for now Jaeden has a cracked skull, broken cheekbone, and there's some swelling on the brain."

"That's a lot of information he got." Penelope slipped onto the stool next to his. She cupped her mug of tea between her palms.

"I get the feeling this isn't over yet." He popped a piece of banana bread into his mouth. "It won't be over until Dawson is caught, and we know beyond doubt both of you are safe."

They needed this time. Joshua deftly adjusted the rope harness, a simple x on Amelia's shoulders and torso. Per her usual, she was naked, and he paused long enough to press a kiss to her neatly trimmed mons. She shivered as he wound the satiny soft rope around her thighs and calves. Once more checking that the knots were tight and wouldn't press on any pressure points, he attached the trailing ends to the star carabiner of the free-standing rope for that purpose.

Amelia brushed a wisp of hair from her face. "We need this," she stated.

Heat enveloped her as he pulled her close. She loved the texture of his clothes against the sensitive skin. She allowed a moan to ease past her lips as she was lifted. For a moment, she experienced weightlessness and disorientation as she swayed.

"Relax, Lia," he soothed, pinching one nipple.

The slight bite of pain morphed into pleasure. She sank into the sensation. Here she was at her most vulnerable, and she felt the safest she had in days. In this room, with him, nothing could hurt her. She wasn't blind, or grieving, or even worried. She just had to embrace the pleasure/pain, and he never stopped touching her.

Amelia soaked up every caress, nip, kiss, pinch, and bite. The burn of the rope only added to the myriad of pleasure. And when he slipped inside her, she came so hard she forgot she was suspended in rope with nothing but air and his hands to keep her anchored to the real world.

Joshua loved taking Amelia like this. So warm and pliant, she wrapped around him like a silken glove. She was so tight and wet for him; it was like the first time all over again. He'd only wanted to tease and arouse her, but the need to claim her, possess her, was too strong to ignore. And when she orgasmed, her tight muscles clamped down and milked his cock. Once. Twice. He welcomed the familiar tingle at the base of his spine. Gently he eased from her body, then lowered her to the floor. He settled a fuzzy, soft blanket over her naked form and settled next to her, combing his fingers through the silky tangle of her hair.

They stayed that way for a long time. When she stirred, Joshua began to remove the ropes from her body. Each one he coiled and tossed aside before moving to the next. Once she was freed, he carefully massaged her limbs. The deep grooves from the ropes would stay for a day or two. Other than that, no damage was done. He scooped her into his arms and carried her to their bed.

"Amazing," she slurred.

He grinned. "As always." He leaned in to kiss her. "Rest. I'll bring some water."

By the time Joshua returned with the promised water, Amelia was fast asleep. He set the bottle on the nightstand, then removed the letter from the drawer.

Back against the headboard and one hand on Amelia, he read the letter.

> Joshua,
>
> If you're reading this, then the world believes me to be dead. This was the only way I could think of to return you back to Amelia and have happiness for myself.
>
> Don't let Amelia grieve for me or Victor. We are together, and we're happy. Hopefully, you won't think me too cruel for letting Amelia and my family believe me dead. As you probably know and have thwarted, Amelia's sister, along with Dawson Cahill,

and that Chad from the firm conspired to swindle Amelia out of her fortune. Dawson also tried to exhort Victor into thinking he was Gage's father. Needless to say, none of it is true. Gage is a Bedford through and through. However, if you need any more evidence on Dawson, look in the locket you gave Amelia. You'll have everything you need to put him away. Keep Amelia safe and happy,

Regards, Gareth

Chapter Twelve

Joshua re-read the letter before he focused on the date it had been written, nearly six months ago. Somehow Gareth had made his way onto the property and placed this letter in the safe. Tomorrow, Joshua would have to go back to the cottage and find out if there was a way to bypass the locks. There had to be if Gareth had placed this letter inside.

And how had Joshua not known Gareth or Victor were dead? Joshua had seen the bodies of both men and attended both funerals. What was worse, Gareth had now burdened Joshua with keeping his secret. He didn't like keeping secrets from Amelia, but he couldn't tell her Gareth and Victor were alive.

Soft lips brushed his thigh. "What's matter?"

Joshua set the letter aside. He settled down in the bed, drawing Amelia in his arms. "Just thinking of the best way to keep you safe," he murmured.

"Don't let me go."

Joshua smoothed her hair from her face, but she was already asleep again. Of course, he wouldn't let her go. She was his everything, and he would die to protect her.

Dawson Cahill was growing more desperate. Thanks to Jaeden, Dawson had a place to sleep, but also thanks to Jaeden's ineptness, Dawson didn't have the money or documents he needed to leave the country. Even the snippets of news he'd heard had his face plastered on every news channel at least once an hour. If he didn't get out of this city, or even the state, soon, he would be found and imprisoned again.

He shuddered. He couldn't go back to that place, not with its communal showers, open toilets, and leering filth just waiting for him to slip up. No, he had to get the money he needed, no, was entitled to and get out of the country. He could make it across the Canadian border without anyone being wiser. From there, he could go to Asia or Europe or that tiny island he'd been planning to hide away in.

Now he was ducking the law and strapped for cash. He could switch focus, perhaps go after the bakery owner. Hadn't Mr. VIP said the other was wealthy as well? Didn't her bakery bring in almost seven figures a year?

Dawson shook his head. He'd been to PB&J Bakery. The location was too open, too busy, and not only would he have to contend with the local police, but there were also security guards. And Gage knew him on sight.

Dawson paced up and down. He could snatch Avery again, but the man was never alone. He was either with an older man or followed by a guard. If he made a try for the blind redhead, that wouldn't work. If Avery was never alone, then Penelope was surrounded by people too. Whenever she was at the bakery, even more security seemed to be around.

If he couldn't get to the baker and his wife, maybe he could get to Joshua a different way.

A cold, feral smile split Dawson's face. There was still one Bedford he could hurt.

"Are you sure the cake is centered?" Penelope carefully placed the molded chocolate roses along the winding staircase between the fragrant sweet layers of cake.

Gage chuckled. "I promise the cake is centered. I made sure each tier was placed on the correct marks. Avery double checked my work."

"I don't mean to be so scattered, but this contract is a big deal." She ran her fingertips across the braille on the box, then reached for another. "If the hotel likes what we do with this function, they'll contract with us for all of the baked goods, which includes items for their banquets, weddings and other functions."

Gage touched her hand. "Relax. The cake is beautiful, and once we finish getting the flowers arranged, people will think the cakes are floating on flowers."

Penelope worried her lip as she placed the flowers on the designated spots. She did this by feel. Each of the different colored flowers were placed in separate boxes, and their corresponding letter was embossed on the stairs and stands for the cake.

"What you do is so impressive and amazing," Gage praised, his tone almost reverent. "They're going to love this."

Penelope cleared the empty boxes into the bags they'd brought in.

"Hold on, P." Gage cleared the rest of the debris while Penelope arranged a rope of greenery.

"I'll get a few pictures, and then we're good to go."

Penelope listened to the shutter snap of Gage's camera phone while she rested her hands on the utility cart with the rest of their tools. At the gasp of surprise, Penelope turned.

"Ms. Bishop, it's remarkable!" A gritty, high-pitched voice announced. "It's Belinda. Are you sure the cake is edible?"

Penelope grinned. "Absolutely. Everything on the cake is edible, including the garland."

An envelope was pressed into her hand.

"You and your bakery have certainly outdone yourselves," Belinda said. "Expect to hear more from me by the end of the week."

"Thank you, Belinda." Penelope smiled as she held to the handle of the cart. Gage maneuvered from the front, giving any who watched the appearance that Penelope was steering.

"I believe congratulations are in order," Gage said once they were outside.

Penelope released an excited squeal. "I can't wait until we get back to the bakery and tell Avery. He'll be so excited."

Gage chuckled as they stowed the gear in the back of the bakery van. "Not that you're excited about the new business."

Penelope laughed, then winced as a sharp wind stung her face. "This cold!" She trailed her fingers along the side of the van until she found the second set of door handles. She opened the door and swung into the passenger seat at the same time Gage occupied the driver's side. The doors slammed one after another.

"You're used to being in the hot box of your kitchen." He cranked the engine.

"Well, if things were so crazy, I'd have walked the cake over instead of having you or someone else drive. The hotel is like two blocks from the bakery."

Gage snorted. "Avery's right; you are stubborn and independent."

"Two of my finest traits," she said with an easy smile.

"Hold on!"

Before Penelope could ask why, metal crashed into metal. The seatbelt tightened a moment before the van tilted. Someone screamed as glass imploded and rained over the occupants. A horn blared before everything went black.

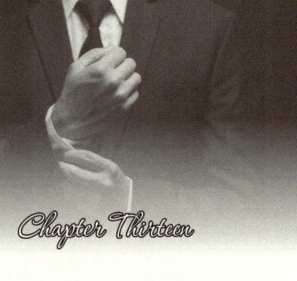

Chapter Thirteen

"Where is she?" Avery demanded, pushing his way through the crowd of people. He'd heard the subsequent squeal of brakes and the loud bang. He'd left the bakery in time to see a pickup truck plow into the side of the bakery van.

He was oblivious to the cold wind whipping through his clothes and fluttering the apron at his waist. He had to get to Penelope.

By the time he reached her side, an EMT had Penelope shrouded in a blanket, sitting on the curb with a patch of gauze to her forehead.

"I don't know what happened," she was saying. "I'm blind!"

"Were you driving?"

Avery would've laughed at the question if he wasn't so shaken. "Of course, she wasn't driving!" he snapped. "She has very limited vision."

"An ambulance will be here shortly," the paramedic stated. "She was unconscious when we moved her from the vehicle."

Avery glanced at the van. "Where's Gage?"

Sirens announced the approach of emergency personnel. Avery pulled out his phone and typed a message he hoped to never have to send.

"I'll meet you at the hospital, P." Avery ran back to the bakery.

⁌

Gage had a moment of disorientation. One moment he was in a van; now he was sitting in a chair. The chair wasn't the heated leather seat of the bakery van, but a hard, uncomfortable, high back wooden thing. His head pulsed in time to his heartbeat. For a moment, the pain was the only thing he could focus on. Something warm and sticky trickled down the corner of his eye. Carefully, he eased open his eyes. Light lanced his pupils and speared through his head. Groaning, he quickly closed them.

"Ah. You're awake."

Gage froze. He knew that pompous, cultured voice. "Seriously?" he pushed as much derision in his voice as possible. "Now you're kidnapping me?"

"I never liked your impudent air," Dawson sneered.

Despite his bounds, Gage looked the other man up and down, as if he were filth. "Firing you was the best thing I ever did. You were a terrible house manager." Gage didn't see Dawson move, but he felt the blow the man dealt. Pain and blackness danced along already overtaxed nerve endings. It took every ounce of will power Gage possessed not to succumb to the sweet oblivion beckoning.

He drew in several deep breaths. Not only did it push away the pain, but it cleared the cobwebs from his addled brain. He wouldn't give into the fear beating at him.

Giving into the emotion would be his downfall. Instead, he masked the feeling with contempt.

"You are nothing more than a coward who bullies and kills those weaker than you. You murdered my brother, for what? Money. Money you were not entitled to."

"Oh, but you're wrong. I earned every dollar cleaning up your parents' messes and then keeping tabs on you. You might have the last name Bedford, but you're not one. That should be enough to keep scandal at bay." He leaned close to Gage. "How much will Amelia pay to keep her husband's name in good standing? Or how much would your parents pay to keep the true nature of your birth secret? Or that the face of Bedford Limited was gay and kept a lover?"

Gage cocked his head to the side, as if considering the situation. "Amelia would tell you to drop dead. She didn't care about Gareth being gay, and Victor is not my father."

Taken aback, Dawson straightened.

Gage flashed a smirk. "The thing about secrets is you have to be sure the person who has the secret really doesn't want it shared." He glowered at Dawson. "That's why my parents spend so little time here. That's why Gareth lived the way he did. He didn't care who knew his sexuality, and I don't care if you say I'm Victor's son. People know you're a murderer and did your best to defraud a blind woman. You're pathetic."

Dawson whipped out a gun. "We'll see just how much your life is worth."

"You're not doing this," Joshua snapped.

"Don't tell me what I'm not doing. Tell me what needs to be done instead," Amelia countered. "Gage is my responsibility."

"And you're mine! You're not delivering the ransom."

"I'm not losing another family member," she told him. "Not when we can do something about it."

"Amelia."

"Joshua!" she countered. "Dawson slammed into the van with Penelope, who is pregnant, and kidnapped Gage. Since Dawson can't get to me or you, he got to Gage."

"Avery says Penelope and the baby are fine," he reminded her.

"That's not the point," she argued. "The point is Dawson is going to keep coming at us or our friends. He has to be stopped."

"On that, we agree."

Amelia paced back and forth. Ever since she got the news about Gage and Penelope, she tried every argument she could to persuade Joshua to take her with him. Putting her in danger was not something her husband would willingly do, but she had to do something. She couldn't let Dawson kill Gage, not when Gareth had already sacrificed his life to keep them both safe.

"Use me as a distraction," she pleaded. "Dawson always thought I was useless and helpless. He always underestimated me."

Joshua crossed to her and placed his hands on her shoulders. "Sweetheart, I know what you're doing. I know you're capable of defending yourself and others, but for my peace of mind, I need you out of harm's way."

She swiped at the tears washing her cheeks. "What's the use of having all this money if all it does is cause issues?"

He kissed her. "Because you have it and they don't. You never wanted the wealth, and they don't know how to live within their means." He kissed her again. "I promise I will bring Gage home."

Chapter Fourteen

"You know his plan isn't going to work," Darius said two hours later.

Amelia stared in the general direction of the speaker. "Of course it will." She'd listened to Joshua and Kota go over a few different plans to rescue Gage. The two men were so thorough, their contingency plans had contingencies. In the meantime, Amelia was forced to sit with a security guard she barely knew.

Darius was pleasant enough, but there was just something a little off about him. She wasn't sure if it was because he was being overly friendly or trying so hard to put her at ease. Whatever it was, it left her off-balance and uneasy. She clicked her tongue and Kiska pushed her cold, wet nose against Amelia's elbow. "Hey girl." Just having the animal close to her eased some of the tension from her body.

Kiska leaned into her, as if sensing Amelia needed the comfort.

"I've watched you for a while now," Darius began conversationally. "You walk around here like not having vision doesn't bother you. If I hadn't seen it for myself, I'd swear you can see."

Amelia frowned. *Is this some kind of backhanded compliment?* "I've been blind my entire life. I know no other way to live."

"Getting close to you has been a real challenge," he continued. "Having to wait until the time was just right to spring our little trap."

A frisson of fear wormed its way down her spine. Kiska must have felt her apprehension. The dog's hackles raised.

A quiet snick had Kiska growling.

"She really is a beautiful animal, but if she attacks me, I will shoot her," Darius promised.

"Quiet," Amelia said. Beside her, Kiska quivered but was silent. "What is it you want?"

"I want to watch Joshua's face when I kill you." Clothing rustled and the furniture creaked as Darius stood. "On your feet, Amelia."

Slowly she did as she was told.

"Now leash your dog."

Amelia shifted, placing her body between her guide and Darius.

He laughed. "You'd seriously take a bullet for that flea bag?"

Amelia lifted her chin. "We're a team, and she's saved my life more than once." Amelia listened hard, straining her ears for every bit of sound. She held her breath, waiting for the movement that would clue her into where Darius's arm was positioned. She caught a flicker of movement and sprang forward.

She grabbed the wrist holding the gun at the same time Kiska latched onto Darius's leg. The man howled with pain. With his free hand, he struck Amelia on the cheek.

Pain exploded in her head, and she loosened her grip, but forced a knee into his solar plexus.

Darius shifted, clipping the sofa. Off balance, he went down, carrying Amelia and Kiska with him. His finger spasmed Amelia cried out as heat singed her arm. Kiska emitted a high-pitched yelp.

"Damn it!"

"Kiska!" Amelia cried, reaching for the whining dog.

"Oh no, you don't!" Darius snatched Amelia up by her hair. The dog growled. "Call her off, or I swear to God, I'll kill her."

Amelia placed a trembling hand, palm out down, at her side. "Stay," she ordered.

"Now. Let's go!" Darius jerked Amelia forward, his hand closed over the wound in her bicep. She gritted her teeth at the pain. Quickly, he bound her wrists in a pair of zip ties. He pushed her out of the house and into the passenger seat of his car.

"Where are you taking me?" She clenched her jaw to stop her teeth from chattering. It was a losing battle until he turned the heat on in the vehicle.

"One last family reunion."

⤴

The cell phone vibrated in Joshua's pocket. He paused long enough to read the display. Frowning, he answered the phone. "This isn't a good time, Time."

"Amelia's in trouble," he said without preamble.

Joshua stiffened. "What do you mean? She's at home with protection."

"I had a vision, Hastings. She's in trouble."

"I'll call her and find out what's going on." Joshua hung up, then dialed Amelia's number. No answer. He dialed Darius's number. He answered after three rings. "Where's Amelia?"

"She's a little busy."

Joshua forced calm he didn't feel and listened. There was wind, muffled thumps, a horn blaring. "Where are you? What's going on?"

"Something happened to Kiska. I'm taking them to the vet."

That could be why Amelia wasn't answering her phone. Kiska was Amelia's constant companion and if the dog was hurt or injured, Amelia would focus all her attention on the animal. "What's wrong with the dog?"

"Not sure, but as soon as we get to the vet, I'll have her call you."

"Do that." Joshua hung up the phone, replaced it in his pocket. Something about the way Darius sounded bothered him. He shook it off. "Kota. I'm going in," he murmured.

"Copy that."

Joshua stepped onto the porch, turned the knob, and walked in. His footsteps echoed on the marble tile as he walked through the long foyer.

"Back here," a cultured voice called out.

Joshua followed the voice until he came to a back bedroom. Dawson stood behind Gage, a gun pointed at the young man's head.

"You know this is a trap," Gage said.

"Of course."

"How's Penelope?" Concern clouded the young man's eyes. "Please tell me she's all right."

"As touching as this is, I have a gun to your head."

Gage rolled his eyes. "He thinks he's in control of this situation."

Joshua lifted a brow. "I see that."

Light swung through the covered window.

"There's a SUV pulling into the drive," Kota announced.

Joshua gave no indication he'd heard the vehicle approach. "For a while there, I thought Rodney was the mastermind behind all this, but I kept wondering why he would break you out of prison, Dawson."

The thin man smiled. "Oh, Rodney and I go way back. I helped him plant the snake in Amelia's wardrobe. If you hadn't been so quick, she'd have died from a snake bite."

Joshua nodded. "Thought so. I'm going to reach for my phone so I can make the transfer."

"Don't do it!" Gage snapped.

"It's only money," Joshua answered.

"Do it slowly," Dawson cautioned.

Nodding, Joshua used his forefinger and thumb to remove his phone. "I'm pulling up the account now." He held the phone so Dawson could see the account balance.

A sickening thud floated through the earpiece, and it took every ounce of self-control Joshua possessed not to react. Something was very wrong. He knew he was in trouble when Gage's eyes flicked to something beyond Joshua's shoulder, and he opened his mouth.

Some instinct had Joshua diving to the side. He caught Gage and toppled the chair. Dawson flew back, and an obscene third eye appearing on his forehead.

Joshua rolled, bringing his weapon up, and stopped cold.

"I wouldn't do that if I were you," Darius said in a sing-song voice.

Joshua took in the forming bruise on Amelia's face and the blood on her clothes, but he did not lower his weapon. Behind him, Gage squirmed. The chair had broken, and Gage was working on freeing himself.

"You never realized who I was," Darius said. "It was too easy getting a job with your firm, then getting close to your family." He squeezed the trigger a mere breath from Gage's outstretched hand before he pressed the still-smoking barrel to Amelia's side. "Tell your little friend to stay still, or I put a bullet through her lungs."

"Gage," Joshua warned.

"Yeah. I got it."

"A life for a life. Is that how it goes? You let my brother die, so I take the life of your wife."

Joshua blinked. He had no idea who Darius was talking about. He'd lost men under his command on his last mission, the same one where he'd been injured, but he hadn't let anyone die, not unless it was one of the civilian casualties.

"Your brother was one of the potentates," he surmised.

"You were supposed to keep him alive!" Darius shouted for the first time, losing control. "He was a hero, and you let him die."

Amelia shifted, whimpering as the gun dug into her ribs. Darius jerked her back in place.

Amelia was tapping her leg.

"I need to scratch my nose," Gage said suddenly. "Is it okay if I scratch my nose? I don't want to get shot for scratching my nose."

"What?"

At the same time, Amelia went slack. The move was so unexpected, Darius was caught off-guard. Gunshots rang out, and it was a moment before Joshua realized there were two different shots. All he registered was Amelia hitting the floor.

Epilogue

Three days later

"I can't believe he shot Kiska," Joshua stroked the Lab, as she laid between him and Amelia. The back left flank was shaved and held several stitches from the bullet graze. A doughnut was around the dog's neck to keep her from licking the wound. "And you were shot too."

Amelia touched the bandage on her arm, seventeen stitches to close the groove. She couldn't remember the last time she'd been in so much pain but worrying whether or not Kiska was alive had been the hardest thing.

"Maybe we should close up shop," Kota said. "Neither one of us caught onto Darius's background."

"Who was he?" Amelia asked, feeding Kiska a treat.

"My last mission, I was sent to guard a group of civilians. They were CEOs who wanted to expand their businesses into a region of the world that isn't fond of westerners. The local regime made their displeasure known with an ambush and a couple of roadside bombs," Joshua explained wearily. "One died, while the other three escaped with injuries. Two of my soldiers were killed and the rest of us wounded."

"Is there any chance of Darius escaping?" Amelia wanted to know.

"He will be in a special wing of a super max facility," Joshua said.

"And in a wheelchair for the rest of his life."

While the bullet Joshua fired hadn't killed Darius, it nicked part of Darius's spine. He probably would have survived that bullet, but it was the bullet fired from Kota's weapon that ensured the man would be a paraplegic.

"I've brought company," Gage announced. "And there's chocolate."

"I love chocolate." Amelia grinned.

"Coming in for a hug," Penelope announced, enveloping Amelia.

"I'm so glad you're okay."

"We're fine, just some bumps and bruises." Penelope assured her. She placed a box in Amelia's hands. "Although I will have to shorten my hours at the bakery now. But enough about me. How are you and Kiska?"

"She's soaking up all the attention she can," Amelia answered. "In a few weeks, Kiska will be good as new."

"She is such a brave girl."

"What happened to the other guy?"

"Jaeden will face his time in prison once he's released from the hospital," Avery supplied.

Amelia nodded. She touched Penelope's hand.

"Let's give them some privacy," Joshua said.

A moment later, only the women remained in the room.

"How are you really doing?" Amelia asked quietly. "Is the baby all right?"

"Still sore and a little rattled but hanging in there. We're having twins."

"Oh, that's wonderful!"

"You could say the accident was a blessing in disguise." She sighed. "It would help to talk to someone about all this. Avery won't admit it, but he has nightmares."

"Understandable. I do have the name of a good therapist."

"That would be great."

"Twins, huh?"

Penelope laughed. "The best surprise ever."

Author Bio

Lynn Chantale, a romance novelist, short story writer, and part-time background singer, has published many stories across several genres. Her works include *Sex, Lies, and Joysticks*, *True Detective Series,* and *Broken Lens,* to name a few.

When she's not actively planning world domination, she's dominating her household, family, and her cat: Shakespeare. You can visit her at any of her cyber haunts:

Website:
https://www.thehouseoflynn.com

Twitter:
https://twitter.com/lynnchantale

Facebook:
https://www.facebook.com/LynnChantaleAuthor

Facebook Group Tale's Tells:
https://www.facebook.com/groups/talestells

Instagram:
https://www.instagram.com/lynn_chantale/

Youtube:
https://www.youtube.com/channel/UCHbAParOHDB7cwfSwUtU3cA

Book Club Questions

1. This book features disabled characters who are thriving in a sighted world. What does this say about disability and the way it is treated in today's world?

2. Revenge is a prominent theme in this series. What do you think about Mr. VIP's motivation for revenge? In what ways, if any, is he justified? What about his companions--do their reasons justify their behavior in any way? What would justify their behavior?

3. The book title acts as a tiny spoiler, giving away the plot. What do you think of the title of this book? What would you have named it? Why?

4. What part of this book was your favorite? Why? What part did you least enjoy? Why?

5. If you were a character in this book, what would you have done differently? Why?

More books from 4 Horsemen Publications

Erotica

Ali Whippe
Office Hours
Tutoring Center
Athletics
Extra Credit
Financial Aid
Bound for Release
Fetish Circuit
Now You See Me
Sexual Playground
Swingers
Discovered

Aria Skylar
Twisted Eros

Chastity Veldt
Molly in Milwaukee
Irene in Indianapolis
Lydia in Louisville
Natasha in Nashville
Alyssa in Atlanta
Betty in Birmingham
Carrie on Campus
Jackie in Jacksonville

Dalia Lance
My Home on Whore Island
Slumming It on Slut Street
Training of the Tramp
The Imperfect Perfection
Spring Break
72% Match
It Was Meant To Be…
Or Whatever

Honey Cummings
Sleeping with Sasquatch
Cuddling with Chupacabra
Naked with New Jersey Devil
Laying with the Lady in Blue
Wanton Woman in White
Beating it with Bloody Mary
Beau and Professor Bestialora
The Goat's Gruff
Goldie and Her Three Beards
Pied Piper's Pipe
Princess Pea's Bed
Pinocchio and the Blow Up Doll
Jack's Beanstalk
Pulling Rapunzel's Hair
Curses & Crushes

Nick Savage
The Fairlane Incidents
The Fortunate Finn Fairlane
The Fragile Finn Fairlane
Us Of Legendary Gods
So We Stay Hidden
The West Haven Undead

Nova Embers

A Game of Sales
How Marketing Beats Dick
Certified Public Alpha (CPA)
On the Job Experience
My GIF is Bigger than Your GIF

Power Play
Plugging in My USB
Hunting the White Elephant
Caution: Slippery When Wet

LGBT Erotica

Dominic N. Ashen
Steel & Thunder
Storms & Sacrifice
Secrets & Spires
Arenas & Monsters
My Three Orc Dads: a Novella

A Breach in Confidentiality
Back Door Pass
My European Adventure
An Unexpected Affair
Finding True Love

Eskay Kabba
Hidden Love
Not So Hidden

Leo Sparx
Before Alexander
Claiming Alexander
Taming Alexander
Saving Alexander
The Case of Armando

Grayson Ace
How I Got Here
First Year Out of the Closet
You're Only a Top?
You're Only a Bottom?
I Think I'm a Serial Swiper
Lookin in All the Wrong Places
What Makes Me a Whore?

Robert Lewis
Someone to Love
Someone to Come Home To

Romance

Ann Shepphird
The War Council

Emily Bunney
All or Nothing
All the Way

All Night Long: Novella
All She Needs
Having it All
All at Once
All Together
All for Her

CPSIA information can be obtained
at www.ICGtesting.com
Printed in the USA
BVHW051243041122
651158BV00004B/1011